HIT WOLF₂

Fred Adams Jr.

AIRSHIP 27 PRODUCTIONS

HITWOLF 2
© 2016 Fred Adams Jr.

Published by Airship 27 Productions
www.airship27.com
www.airship27hangar.com

Interior illustrations © 2016 Clayton Hinkle
Cover illustration © 2016 Zachary Brunner

Editor: Ron Fortier
Associate Editor: Steve BennettMarketing and Promotions Manager: Michael Vance
Production and design by Rob Davis.

ISBN-10: 0-9977868-3-3
ISBN-13: 978-0-9977868-3-5

Printed in the United States of America

10 9 8 7 6 5 4 3 2 1

HITWOLF₂

Fred Adams Jr.

I

24 October 1969
Chambliss, Georgia
Moonrise.

"Billy, change the tape. Put in Vanilla Fudge," Roxanne Barton whispered in Billy's ear.

"Sure, Roxy, whatever you want." Billy Davis leaned over her and pulled out the eight-track tape of Led Zeppelin II. He hated Vanilla Fudge; he always liked the Supremes' version of "You Keep Me Hangin' On" and didn't understand why a bunch of dopers had to screw it up. For that matter, he didn't like Led Zeppelin either, but Roxy did, and he wanted to get laid.

Billy Maxwell, seventeen years old, captain of the Chambliss Chiefs baseball team, headed for OSU on a baseball scholarship next year, and still a virgin. He asked Roxy out on a date because he thought she might come across for him.

Roxy was a sophomore and wanna-be hippie who wore little square sunglasses and tie-dyed caftans over her bell-bottomed jeans. She said things like, "oh wow," and "right on," and flashed everybody the two finger peace sign like the hand on the old Kendall motor oil signs you still saw with bullet holes in them along the side of the road or nailed to the wall of some gas station in the sticks.

Billy didn't tell anybody he was going out with her; she wasn't a cheerleader or even a majorette or even that good looking. Actually, she was kinda chunky and her hair frizzed out like a giant Brillo pad, but when she walked, Billy could see she didn't wear a bra under that tie dye. That's why he invested fifty cents in the condom machine at the gas station and that's why he and she were making out on a Friday night in the front seat of his dad's Pontiac Bonneville on the Knob, a promontory overlooking Chambliss, Georgia.

The Knob was a great big outcrop of limestone with boulders pushing like knuckles through the red dirt. Some enterprising soul had carved the initials LSD in foot-high letters into one of the huge rocks, testimony to the types who frequented the place. In the moonlight, the pines around the boulders cast tar-black shadows over the dun stone. Maybe it was the reefer he smoked with Roxy that made the place look so spooky. The dope cost him plenty, plus he had to venture into dark town to buy it, but he figured if he wanted her to put out, he had to put out a little too.

He found the Vanilla Fudge tape by the green dashboard lights and fumbled for the slot of the Mini-eight. He'd had to almost cut off his right hand to get his dad to allow him to bolt the tape player under the dashboard of his precious Bonneville and the old man wouldn't let him cut holes to put decent speakers in the doors. He had to wire both channels of the player into the crappy factory oval in the dashboard.

Billy was getting a headache. Maybe it was the pot; he'd never smoked it before. Maybe it was the loud music. Maybe it was Roxy's stupid rap about peace, love, and universal consciousness.

He was sliding the tape into the player when Roxy grabbed his hand. "Wait. Billy, what was that?"

"What was what?"

"I heard something."

Sure, Billy thought, I bet you hear things all the time. "I didn't hear anything."

"Weed heightens your senses," she said. "The more you smoke it, the more aware you get. Listen."

Billy listened. He didn't hear a sound. Maybe because of the pot he was a little slow on the uptake, but the thought finally jelled. No sound at all. No crickets, no frogs, no nothing. If it was some of those morons from shop class out to bust his chops, he'd teach them a lesson. Billy reached behind the seat and pulled up his Louisville Slugger. He grabbed for the door handle.

"Hey, where are you going?"

"If somebody's out there, I'm gonna bust his head."

"Billy, don't. I'm scared. Let's just leave."

Now Billy was royally pissed off, and that overrode common sense. Whoever was messing up his big chance was going to pay for it big time. Roxy grabbed his arm. "What if it's somebody dangerous?"

"Oh for Christ's sake," Billy said. "Who do you think it is, the Man With The Hook?" He shook off her arm. "If there's somebody out there spying on us, I'm gonna rap a base hit with his skull." He opened the door and stepped out into the cool October night.

As an afterthought, he turned on the quad headlights. "Okay, asshole, spotlight dance." He swaggered around the front of the car, taking warm up swings with the bat. "You want some, come on out in the light and get it."

He turned from side to side surveying the Knob. Nothing. Nobody. When he got back in the car, Roxy better be ready for him.

Then he saw the pair of eyes glowing gold in the headlights. Slowly, they rose until he saw the furred head, the broad shoulders and the long arms of the intruder.

The werewolf leapt over the boulder with one graceful bound and landed in a crouch ten feet away from Billy. He dropped the bat and would have screamed, but Roxy was already doing it for him.

The beast crept forward slowly, its impossibly long arms spread and its fangs shining in the headlights. The werewolf straightened up and Billy saw it was his height, six-six easy but the creature outweighed Billy by at least fifty pounds. A silver string of drool hung from one side of its maw. A low rumble came from its thick chest as it spread its claws.

A blur of motion flew from the left and the werewolf toppled to one side. Billy stared open-mouthed in shock. It was another werewolf like the first. The pair rolled on the ground snapping and snarling, neither giving any quarter. Seconds later, a third shape darted into the light from the pines and joined the brawl.

The two newcomers were smaller than the first monster, but they were better fighters. The battle quickly turned against the bigger werewolf and he fled from the clearing. One of the smaller pairs charged after him, but its companion stayed behind. It walked up to the paralyzed boy, made an almost apologetic bow, and said in a guttural, all but unintelligible voice, "Sorry." Then it bounded away after its fellows.

Billy didn't get back in the car for a while. He was waiting for his jeans to dry.

• • •

Two miles away, the three werewolves were still running, the big one in the lead. One of the smaller ones circled left and cut him off at a fork in the forest trail. He tackled the big one who fell face down with a heavy thud. The third werewolf dove onto the big one's back and wrapped a hairy arm around its throat, cutting off its wind. The big one thrashed and flailed, but between the two of them the smaller werewolves subdued it.

The big one relaxed and slapped the ground three times. The two smaller werewolves let him up. One of the smaller ones, the leader, gave an inquisitive snarl and made a gesture with his raised thumb, the black claw gleaming in the moonlight. The Big one looked at the ground until the smaller one backhanded him none too lightly in the chest, repeating the snarl and gesture.

The big one nodded and raised his thumb in acknowledgement. The leader held out his left arm in a handshake position and swung it open-handed from the elbow, waist to shoulder: Come. He turned and loped gracefully down the path. The other two fell in behind and they disappeared into the dark forest.

II

John Slate woke to the squawking of a blue jay outside the window of the cabin. Jays were annoying, but you couldn't be angry with them. They couldn't help themselves. It was just their nature to bully any bird in sight. That didn't stop Slate from hoping that someday, some red-tailed hawk would swoop out of the sky and carry off the jay for good. But today wasn't the day, and Slate was wide awake.

The change back to human was exhausting, although in werewolf form he seemed to have unlimited strength and endurance. Last night was a chore. He had turned Swede, the second member of his team two days before and was guiding him through his period of acclimation, a benefit he didn't have when he was turned less than a year before on the orders of a Jersey gangster named Michael Monzo to make him an enforcement tool for his operation.

Slate had escaped and Monzo and most of his crew were now dead, but life was anything but safe for Slate and his men. They were sold out by the Company and left to fend for themselves in Laos to cover the collective ass of some politicians and were prime targets if the suits in D.C. found out they were even alive let alone in the country. Add to them Elroy Poston the game warden who saw Slate in werewolf form when the team shot it out with three of Monzo's men in the Pine Barrens.

They pinned the dead mobsters on Poston, figuring correctly that he would skate, but Poston didn't seem like the type to let things lie. And there was Bill Hannisford the tabloid photographer whose trip-wire camera caught a shot of Slate in his full-furred glory fleeing a forest fire. He wasn't likely to forget about Slate either.

Slate levered himself off the cot. He picked up his watch where it lay on the table. 0831 hours. Haines and Swede were still asleep. The moon hadn't set until 0542 hours and all three of them were pretty beat after a night in the woods. Singer's cot was empty and Slate smelled coffee. He pulled on his shirt and jeans and ambled to the kitchen.

Singer sat at the kitchen table facing the bedroom door with a cup of coffee in his left hand and a .45 automatic beside his right on the table. Even as he hunched over, his shoulders looked broad and his arms thick. His buzz cut had grown out since they'd set up their compound and it stuck out at all angles like the spines of a sea urchin. "How'd it go, Johnny?"

"It went," Slate said, pouring himself a mug of coffee. It was strong, it was hot, and it was just what Slate needed.

"Is Swede coming around?"

"He's on his way."

When the other members of the team decided that they would become werewolves like their leader, Slate had to think long and hard about the implications and the logistics of the move. Sun-Tzu wrote, "know the other, know the self" but he had no advice for those times when the other becomes the self. Slate remembered all too well the mobster from Monzo's crew who became completely unhinged and all but uncontrollable when he changed and a catatonic vegetable when he was human.

Every person is a wild card, he thought, and there's no telling how anyone might react. Turning them all at once would have been chaotic when the next full moon rose. He decided to turn them one at a time, Haines first.

None of them was unstable, and all of them were fearless, but Haines seemed the best candidate. It turned out he was a good choice. The first time was always a shock no matter how much you've been told or what you've been through in your life. No words could describe the pain of your bones rearranging themselves, of fangs pushing out of your gums, and the spikes of coarse hair sprouting from every pore, or the shock of looking at yourself in a mirror and seeing what you've become.

Likewise, no words could capture the feeling of absolute savage power the new form provided, power enough to tear a world in two with your claws. By the third transition, Haines seemed to take it in stride. He had his emotions and his newly released urges fully in check, and Slate could trust him on his own.

Slate chose Swede as the next to go. Of the three surviving members of his team, Singer seemed to be the most skittish about the business. Slate hoped that the successful conversion of Haines and Swede would give Singer the confidence he needed to take the big step when it was his turn, but he wasn't there yet. The rounds in the .45 had silver slugs.

Slate didn't blame him for his caution, Singer being the only human in the camp outnumbered by three werewolves, and Slate had no plans to push him. But a decision had to be made soon. He or one of the others had to bite Singer while the moon was full for him to turn on the next one. That meant he had two days to decide whether Swede was safe and Singer was ready, or he would have to wait another month before he could turn him.

In some ways it could be useful to have a human on the team with the others turned; for example, Slate still hadn't tried driving the van in werewolf form, but ultimately, team cohesion demanded that they all be in the same boat.

"Two more nights and things go back to normal, huh, Johnny?" Singer said, staring into his coffee cup.

"Yeah, whatever normal means these days." Slate picked up his coffee and pushed open the screen door. The rusted hinges squealed like a pair of shoats. Anybody else would probably oil them, but their signal noise was an early warning of intruders. The moon would start waning Monday, but the *Farmer's Almanac* wasn't quite specific about what time it would technically go out of phase, so they might have a short night or none. He needed a better source of info.

From what he'd learned, interference in the full moon's exposure to the Earth affected the change. A lunar eclipse turned him human then back to a werewolf when the full moon was restored, as he'd discovered in the middle of a battle with Laszlo Kovacs, another werewolf sent to kill Monzo by a mystery man named Greystone. Kovacks, more experienced at fighting as a werewolf, was winning until the eclipse turned them human and he learned that Slate was just as deadly in human form.

The sun shone on the grassy yard in front of the cabin's porch and beyond it the mirror surface of the water. The camp stood on the tip of a peninsula that projected into a lake ringed with cypress trees and choked with lily pads, part of ten thousand acres of marshland. Slate walked to the dock where a swamp skimmer was moored beside a Zodiac inflatable boat.

Across the water, a big gator entered the lake with a heavy splash. The swamp was as remote and desolate a place as he had ever seen and every bit as dangerous as the rice paddies of Viet Nam. Once in a while they could see a skiff across the water or hear the crack of a rifle in the distance, but they rarely saw a soul. For the team, it was as good a hideout as they could want.

He felt a heavy tread on the dock and knew it was Swede without looking. "Hey, Swede, how you feeling?"

"Strung out. My head's a little foggy." The big man sat on the dock beside Slate. Swede was a head taller than Slate and outweighed him by seventy pounds of hard muscle. His beard matched the blonde hair that hung in a thick braid between his shoulder blades. "Otherwise, I'm okay."

"What do you remember from last night?"

"Most of it. I kinda lost it for a while."

"Yeah, things got away from you. We had to rein you in. You almost had some teenager for supper."

He nodded. "Yeah, I remember a little bit of that."

"We were lucky. I smelled reefer pretty strong, and whatever he and his girlfriend saw if they tell anybody will be written off as hallucination or a Halloween prank. But you have to get control of yourself, Swede. If we go out on a mission, Haines and I can't be watching you with one eye."

"I have two more nights this round. I'll work it out."

"No choice, Swede, you're committed. We all are, and we can't run it back."

• • •

Later in the morning, while the others were on a trip into Chambliss for supplies, Slate walked to a spot a hundred yards from the cabin and stopped at the foot of a big cypress tree hung with Spanish moss. A fat copperhead, six feet of pure meanness, slithered over the roots. Slate stood back and waited until it was gone. The snake's nest under the roots was one reason he chose this spot as a secure hiding place. He waited until it was gone before he unfolded a short trenching shovel and dug into the red soil. In a few minutes, he retrieved a square tin box the size of a book, tucked it under his arm and headed back to the cabin.

In the box was an amulet that had been used by the now dead wizard Pegg to control Slate when he was Monzo's pet werewolf. He had thought first to destroy it but realized it may still have use for them in the right hands. What he needed was information on its origin and its function.

He set the box on the table in the kitchen beside a pad of paper and a pencil. Inside the box, the amulet was wrapped in a stained piece of blue terry cloth. Slate lifted it out and thought long and hard before he unwrapped it.

The amulet was heavy, cast from silver, and consisted of snakelike vines twisted into a rough hexagon. The vines were inscribed with runic symbols, and in its center, the amulet held a glowing purple gemstone that pulsed in the sunlight from the windows. As he stared at it, the runes seemed to writhe like living things and he felt himself being drawn into the amulet's violet eye.

Slate threw the cloth over the stone and shook his head to clear it. He uncovered it again and quickly laid the paper over the amulet. With the pencil, he rubbed over the sheet, leaving the amulet's shape and the markings on its surface. When he was finished, he wrapped the amulet again without looking at it and put it back in the box. Two more days, then he could start searching for answers.

III

"Look, Jake, I saw what I saw." Billy paced back and forth across Jake's bedroom, his fists clenching and unclenching. The transistor radio on the nightstand blared like a nest of wasps in a tin can as the Archies sang the praises of "Sugar Sugar."

"God, I hate that song. Can you believe it was number one two weeks ago?" Jake Smalley sat up on the bed. He was the varsity team's catcher and Billy's usual partner in mischief. Short and thick, Jake was the perfect backstop for Billy's wilder pitches. "Okay, let me get this straight. You say you saw a werewolf…"

"No, not 'I say I saw.' Damn it, I saw them, three of them. At the knob."

"I gotta ask, man, how many beers did you have?"

"I didn't have any."

"Oh, yeah, that's right," Jake said, nodding and slowly pushing his lower lip under his upper one thoughtfully. "I forgot you were with Roxy. What I shoulda said was how much wacky weed did you smoke last night?"

"That doesn't matter, Jake. I saw them. So did Roxy."

"Now there's what Perry Mason calls a 'credible witness.'"

Billy threw Jake's catcher's mitt at his head. "Are you gonna take me serious or not?"

"Okay, Billy, take it easy, huh?" Jake stared him down. "Think about it, man. Are you sure it wasn't just some guys dressed up for Halloween?"

"Jake, I swear, they were real."

"I'll take your word for it, but if you expect people to believe you, you need some proof."

"Like what?"

"I don't know, maybe photos."

"Oh, sure, I'm gonna go back up to the Knob and go looking for those werewolves. Maybe they'll pose for me, you think?"

The Archies faded and Tommy James and the Shondells launched into "Ball of Fire."

"Now there's another one I can't stand," Jake said. "Tommy James and the Shondells used to play some decent rock and roll, I mean 'Hanky Panky' was a classic, and now they're doing all that psychedelic peace and love horseshit."

He stood up and shut off the radio. "Let's go up there now, while it's still light and see what's what. You've seen all the movies I have. If they're werewolves, they won't be around until the moon comes up, right? It's supposed to rain tonight, and if there are any tracks now, they won't be there tomorrow.

"The reason I said to bring a camera is this." Jake pulled a magazine from a pile beside the bed. The title emblazoned across the cover in bold yellow letters read: "*Unidentified: Land, Sea, and Space.*" The cover showed a blurry black and white picture of what looked like two hubcaps welded together and the bold caption "Terror in the Texas Skies."

He turned to a back page and pointed to an ad outlined by a thick black bar. It read: "Have you seen a UFO? Have you been abducted by aliens? Have you sighted Bigfoot? Send us your experiences and be featured on our readers' page. $100 if we use your story."

"That kind of cash will buy us lots of beer, Billy."

• • •

In less than an hour, Billy was bouncing on the back of Jake's Yamaha

Bear Scrambler up the rutted road to the Knob, holding the seat strap with one hand and a small knapsack with the other. Jake had borrowed his older sister's Polaroid camera and Billy bought a film pack at the drug store. They could have used Jake's Instamatic, but Jake said that if they did find something worth a picture, why run the risk of some guy in a photo lab stealing it and cashing in on it.

Jake downshifted and the two-stroke engine whined like a chainsaw. The leaves were late turning this year and only now were showing red, yellow and bronze. The late turn meant a change in the weather they would fall quickly, leaving the forest bare, but for the moment it glowed in the late afternoon sun.

In daylight, the Knob looked pleasant, picturesque even, if you overlooked the cigarette butts, beer cans and other rubbish left by the local teens. "Okay, Billy where did you see them?" Jake looked around.

Billy stood in the middle of the clearing. "I was parked here and the first one, the big one came over that rock. He landed right there." Billy pointed to a spot in the grass. "Then one came from that side, I think and the other one from the trees behind you."

Jake stood thinking for a minute. "Too bad he landed in the grass where he wouldn't leave footprints. Let's look around a little maybe there's some soft ground where he left tracks." When nothing turned up in the clearing, Billy and Jake opted to follow the trail the werewolves took when they ran away. "Let's walk it," said Jake. We're not gonna see anything riding the bike."

The trail was a path walked frequently enough to wear it down to hard-packed dirt. Scattered leaves lay along the edges and the ferns and bushes grew inward from both sides almost closing over it. A half mile down the mountain from the Knob, a small stream cut across the trail. Jake crouched down and studied the softer soil beside it. "Look."

Pressed into the dirt was the print of a large foot. Billy whistled. "Looks like at least a size twelve."

The track was essentially human, but where the ball of the foot should have been they saw the shape of an angular pad. At the end of each of the five toes was a deep gouge in the ground. Claws.

"Get out the camera."

IV

Moonrise.

The third night of Swede's initiation, he, Slate and Haines waited on an open patch of ground in the middle of a pine forest a few miles from the swamp. Slate didn't want to risk another night of prowling near Chambliss in case someone took the kid's story seriously.

They sat naked on the grass, their clothes piled neatly out of sight under a shelf of rock. In the distance to the west, flashes of lightning it the sky. The weather forecasts were right. A storm was coming. Slate felt his pulse quickening and stubbed out his unfinished cigarette on the ground. "It's time."

The silver edge of the moon cleared the horizon and the shift began.

When Pegg had used the amulet and Slate was under the wizard's control, the change seemed almost natural, but without its influence, no matter how many times Slate turned from one form to the other the pain was intense. It no longer frightened him, but that didn't stop him from hurting.

The itching erupted over every inch of his body as fish hooks of dark hair thrust through his skin. Slate took deep breaths and sat still, trying to be a good model for the others. Swede groaned through clenched teeth, trying to tough it out as his bones began to shift, his joints reconfiguring themselves, but Slate knew how it hurt. His joints were doing the same thing.

Haines doubled over, vomiting blood as his organs rearranged themselves. Swede rolled onto his back and curled into a ball, his hands clutching his knees as black claws burst like thorns through his fingertips. Slate felt his jaws thrust forward, stretching his face into a grotesque mask. Fangs bored through his gums and finally he let out a howl that was less than human. The others joined in and he realized the transformation was complete for them all.

Slate stood first, then Haines and finally Swede. The change affected shaped each of them differently and made each unique, exaggerating their physical attributes. Haines was a lean, compact man, and his werewolf shape was long limbed and proportioned as if an artist had designed him. Swede, with his thickly muscled torso, sported a cruel set of shoulders that forced his head down and forward while his arms bulged as if they would rupture his pelt at any second.

After raising his head and sniffing the air, Slate snarled, "Okay?"

Haines replied in an equally bestial tone, "Okay."

Swede raised a thumb and nodded his head. He had not yet found his voice and Slate hoped he would soon. Speech was a crucial factor in balancing the animal and the human in the psyche; communication eliminated isolation, something Slate felt intensely when he was first turned. Haines had developed the skill much more quickly than Slate, but unlike Slate, he had the benefit of preparation and explanation to guide him. Pegg had left Slate in the dark, most likely to better control him through fear and uncertainty. Slate wanted every member of the team to be perfectly sure of himself and confident in the others.

He gave the sign to follow and began running west toward the distant lightning. Swede and Haines ran after him, more graceful in their second forms than they were in their first. Swede showed no hesitation or disorientation tonight, which encouraged Slate. He was training them to maneuver, to stalk, to kill as a team with fangs and claws just as he had trained them to do so with weapons and technology.

Once the human side of their minds was secure, Slate counted on the bestial side guiding them by instinct. His job, to temper the two, was a tricky balancing act with a lot of unknown factors. Each human being was unique and his reaction to the irreversible turning was a mine field Slate had to navigate with care. So far, he made it through okay, and so did Haines. Swede was adapting a little slower than Haines had, but he seemed to be coming along.

What haunted Slate was the thought of Monzo's man Tommy Cimino who was turned with no preparation or knowledge and went completely berserk, bouncing off the walls and bars of his cage and howling through the night at an unseen moon. What to do if any of his men went wild was an unresolved question. Imprisoning or restraining him would involve time and attention that would hamper operations.

Killing one may not be as easy as it seemed. To do it with silver, the most effective means would require handling the stuff and poison him as surely as the rogue. When Swede slipped his gears the night before, it took both Slate and Haines to subdue him, and killing him in a one-on-one fight would be a tall order in human or werewolf form. He could only hope that Swede would get control of himself quickly.

The pack ran and they ran and they ran. Clouds slipped over the moon and the steady silver glow was soon replaced by the strobing flash of lightning as the storm truck full force. The rain hammered the earth as if punishing it for some great sin, or perhaps punishing the three dark forms that ran wild through the veil of celestial tears.

The others didn't catch the whiff of scent that Slate did because they hadn't yet learned to use their senses to maximum efficiency. A deer was bedded nearby. Slate wanted to hunt as a team of three as he had hunted prey with Haines the month before to make them think and act in tandem and instead of fighting their primitive instincts, tap into them and make of themselves weapons more formidable than guns or knives could ever be.

Slate grunted and the trio turned as uniformly as a school of fish into the brush.

The deer was a buck, eight points, and a drop tine, waiting out the rain. It was rutting season and the urges were strong, but the heavy rains subdued the scent of does in estrus, so he bedded down until the storm ended. The crashing thunder covered the stealthy creep of the werewolves through the thick foliage and the soggy leaves gave no hint of their approach.

The trio separated and spread for a three-pronged attack. Slate raised a paw and made a horseshoe gesture with it. Advance. He could see the buck in the lightning flashes, bedded down barely concealed in the high grass. Closer. Closer. Slate's heightened hearing picked up the short breaths of the buck and he could almost taste its hot blood and tangy meat.

The deer, spooked by some unknown signal, sprang up and bolted. The werewolves closed on it from three sides, but it vaulted a heavy thicket of brambles and dashed through the dense wet brush. Haines led the chase, following the deer's trail with Slate and Swede crashing through the dense undergrowth behind him.

The deer chose its escape route well. The trail snaked through the thick-boled pines and over fallen trees, rocks, and roots that could break an ankle or worse in the darkness. The sharp bare intertwined lower branches of the pines raked at them, pointed sticks that would have flayed an ordinary human but broke over the thick pelts of the werewolves.

The deer knew the path and its perils. The team did not. They ran in silence over the rough terrain, frustrated that their plan didn't work, but exhilarated by the chase.

The deer broke from the trees and ran at a steep bank over a wide creek bed, a deep cut swelling with water in the heavy rains. Without hesitation, the deer took a running leap across the gulley and landed on the opposite bank, never breaking its stride as it plunged into the dark on the other side.

The team followed. Haines made the jump and cleared the creek with ease. Slate made it across but slipped in the wet grass and fell headlong. In a second he was on his feet again in pursuit. Swede made the leap and barely caught the edge of the bank with his hands. The rain-softened earth gave way and he tumbled backward onto the rocks below. He howled in pain and anger then jumped to his feet and began clawing his way up the steep embankment.

The deer zigzagged through one rugged passage after another until it finally broke cover into an open meadow. It was thirty yards ahead of Slate and Haines and it was tiring, its lead diminishing. They were closing quickly when a bright light flashed across the meadow, a sealed beam spot. As one, Slate and Haines halted. Slate gave the palm down sign to crouch but before they could, shots rang out and the buck went down. Jacklighters.

Two men crossed the meadow toward the fallen deer shining their lights. They were all but indistinguishable in rain ponchos. Both carried high-powered rifles. A part of Slate was furious at these interlopers stealing their prey at the last moment, but another part of him knew that although they could kill these rednecks with ease, their deaths would bring attention they didn't want or need. There may come a time when it wouldn't matter, but that time was not yet.

Slate put a finger in the air and rotated it. Return to the rally point. As silently as shadows they crept from the field into the trees unnoticed by the hunters.

V

Jack Martin and Connor Tate were marveling at their good luck. The buck was a big one and would dress out to a hundred twenty-five pounds easy. The trophy was a nice one too with a drop tine and would fetch a good price as a mount to hang in some restaurant or bar.

"The ground's too soft here for the truck," said Connor. "We'll have to drag him."

Jack nodded. "Yeah, but he's a nice one. I didn't think we'd see much; figured they'd be bedded down for the storm. We got lucky tonight."

"Well, let's not push our luck too far. Shut out the light before somebody sees us out here." Jack slung his rifle over his shoulder, and as he did, he heard a thrashing in the brush at the edge of the field. He quickly unslung his rifle and threw the bolt. "Turn the light over that way," he said quietly. "Now."

The light flashed on and Jack saw a dark shape disappearing into the trees. He snapped off a shot, threw the bolt and fired again. "A bear," he said, and a big one. Come on."

Swede, separated from the others had followed their rain-diluted scent and came onto the meadow. His chest heaved from the hard run through the woods. He saw the hunter's light and smelled the blood of the kill. His instincts told him to attack, to tear the throats from the thieves who took his catch. Then the light shone on him and the other side of his mind said, run.

Two bullets whizzed by him as he tore through the thick undergrowth and back down the trail. Behind him, he could hear the hunters coming even through the pelting rain, their panting breaths, and their clumsy tread. Swede knew they couldn't catch him but didn't slacken his pace. The thought formed in his brain: back to the rally point.

"Damn," said Jack, shining his light around the brush. "I was hoping I got him. He was a big one."

Connor cupped his hand around a Marlboro, shielding the match from the rain. "Well, I guess you didn't. There ain't no tracks and there ain't no blood, so I guess there ain't no bear to take home. Let's get that buck on the truck." Connor chuckled at his rhyme. "Get the goddamned buck on the goddamned truck."

"Yeah, I guess so," said Jack taking one last look around. "Sometimes you get the bear and sometimes the bear gets you. Sometimes neither one, I guess." But this ain't over, mister bear, he thought, not by a stretch.

VI

Slate and Haines crouched under the shelter of an overhang. The rain was still pounding the ground, but the lightning was fading. It was hard to reckon time without the moon as a reference, but Slate figured they had almost two more hours before it set. Swede had not yet returned and Slate was beginning to worry, not that Swede was hurt or dead, but that he would become human again and be found by some hunter or game warden naked and unarmed in the middle of the forest.

In a flash of lightning, Slate saw movement. In the next flash, he recognized the shape. It was Swede. He bounded out to meet him and immediately caught the scent of blood but relaxed when he realized it was Swede's own from cuts and scratches across his muzzle. This time, it was Swede who grunted and gave the thumbs-up. Slate responded in kind and they hunkered down under the rock to wait for the change to begin.

Moonset.

The team said little as they hiked to the van in the pre-dawn light. Coming back always felt like a bad hangover. Taking a cool down period before the change, trying to rest and recover helped, but it was no total solution. Even when Pegg controlled the changes with the amulet, Slate felt wrung out when he woke.

The return was always a mixed bag for Slate. On one hand, he was relieved to be human again, on the other, he lamented the loss of the enhanced vitality that not only allowed but encouraged physical activity that pushed every limit. The feeling of absolute power, of savage freedom, could be as addictive as any drug and Slate understood it had the potential to be as enslaving as heroin. A part of him was glad it could happen only four times a month, but a darker part of him wished it could be always.

When the team arrived at the cabin, Singer was keeping his vigil. Swede and Haines shambled off to the bedroom and in minutes, both were snoring. Slate slumped into a chair opposite Singer.

"Good night?"

Slate nodded. "Yeah, I think Swede has a handle on it."

"Good news."

Neither of them wanted to broach the subject, and Slate was too beat for the discussion. "Yep. Tonight should do it for him." He stretched and yawned and started to get up from the table when Singer stopped him.

"I've been thinking a lot about turning, Johnny," he said, wrapping his hands around his coffee. "Tonight's the night, huh?"

Slate sat back in his chair. "It's a big move. Once it's done, you can't put the shit back in the goose."

Singer stared at the end of his cigarette. "I don't know, man. I keep thinking about Faro and Hitch, dead because of the neckties in D.C. I feel

"I've been thinking...about turning, Johnny."

like I owe it to them to make the move."

"I've been thinking about it too. When the moon comes up, no matter how disciplined we become, we're still going to need a pair of human hands on things from a logistical point of view."

"A Renfield, huh?"

"Renfield?"

Singer grinned with the corner of his mouth. "You don't know Renfield?"

Slate shook his head.

"Ever see the movie *Dracula*? Renfield's the ops guy who takes care of business while Dracula's taking his daily dirt nap."

Slate looked at the automatic lying next to Singer's right hand then into Singer's eyes. "You'd be okay with that on an operation, human while we aren't?"

Singer took a long drag on his cigarette. The smoke dribbled from the corners of his mouth. "How many times have you saved my life, Johnny, and how many times have I saved yours?"

"Who's counting?"

"My point exactly. I trust you, John. I trust you as a team leader, and I trust you as my friend. I'm good either way, turn me or don't."

"So you're cool with staying human for now?"

"What did you always teach us, Johnny? What we want comes in fourth place after the mission, the mission, and the mission. You know, in some ways I envy you. You didn't have to agonize over this crap; it just happened. In another month, we'll be having this conversation again."

"Not unless you bring it up." Slate stood. "I need some sleep."

Slate landed on his cot fully clothed and was out in seconds.

VII

Elroy Poston was unpacking his duffel bag; a week's worth of clean clothes from his trip to the Laundromat. His clothes were nearly all he had left after he paid his lawyers. His new rented room was cramped and dingy, and sported a view of a brick wall outside its one window, but the rent was a hell of a lot lower than his old apartment. The lawyers had cost him plenty, but he finally walked on the shooting of the three mobsters in the

Pine Barrens. The State Police detectives, Nichols, and Parks should have been happy the gangsters were dead, and they might have left him alone if the rest of Monzo's crew hadn't been killed in a shootout the next night and Monzo himself killed in a fire that screamed arson in his nightclub.

Poston admitted the whole thing looked like a conspiracy, but damn it all, he wasn't a part of it, he was just a park warden doing his job. The Jersey State Police and the FBI didn't agree. Tom Barnett, his boss stood by him through the trial, but when it was over, he let Poston know that his time was up.

He cashed in his G. I. insurance and his pension account to pay off the lawyers and to give him enough bucks to buy what he needed. The HR trank rifle lay disassembled in its case. Beside it sat the starlight scope an Army Ranger buddy from his old unit pilfered from Camp Merrill. It was time to go hunting. Poston didn't know where just yet, but if he hung in, he'd find his quarry and prove once and for all he was right. Plenty of time, he thought. I have the rest of my life.

VIII

Slate woke past noon, alone in the cabin. He didn't ordinarily sleep so late but the last few nights were particularly taxing, physically and mentally. The coffee was cold in the tin campfire pot, so he lit a burner on the propane stove. While it heated, he splashed cold water on his face at the kitchen sink.

All the comforts of home, he thought. The team bought the hunting camp two years before as a stateside hideout. The compound was eighteen miles from the nearest town. Surrounded by a swamp full of alligators and cottonmouth water moccasins on three sides and accessible only by a rutted mud pit of a road on the fourth, it was as good a place as any to hole up.

The cabin was crude by home standards, but compared to sleeping in a wallow in a rice paddy, it was the Taj Mahal. The walls were rough pine planking with open joists inside and a tin roof that made the heavy Georgia rain sound like buckshot. A river stone fireplace kept the interior warm and a kerosene generator kept the lights burning. All in all, the right place for the moment.

Slate was pouring his coffee when the screen door screeched and Haines strolled in. "Done with your beauty sleep, huh?"

"I wish. Every time I wake up, I look in the mirror and don't see any difference. Lost cause. Where are the others?"

"Swede's in the water fixing something on the airboat and Singer's handing him the tools." Haines poured out the last of the coffee and sprawled on a chair. "He did better last night."

Slate nodded. "He'll be all right." He paused. "I decided to hold up turning Singer."

Haines nodded, staring at nothing, but Slate could tell his gears were turning. "So is this a permanent decision or open to revision?"

"For now. Between us, I don't think he's ready for it. Besides, somebody has to drive the van and be a face man when the moon's up."

Haines chuckled. "Oh, a Renfield."

Slate rolled his eyes. "Am I the only person who never saw that movie?"

Haines's face went serious. "For what it's worth, Johnny, I agree with the decision. I think Singer's been half afraid of turning all along, and even after three months exposed to it, he's still nervous around us when we turn. Maybe later it'll be different. So what's the agenda?"

"Tonight we finish Swede's initiation." Slate looked through the window at nothing in particular. "Tomorrow we start planning."

IX

Langley, Virginia

"So tell me about Slate." Carlton Briggs leaned back in his chair and propped his feet on the desk, setting the heels of his wingtips on a blue folder with a State Department seal on the cover and the words "Eyes Only."

Tom MacDonald shrugged. He sat in a hard, straight-backed chair in front of the arrogant, monolithic prow of Briggs's desk like a teenager in the principal's office. Briggs's chair was high-backed, upholstered and comfortable. The power office message was clear: I'm the King. The arrogant gesture of showing MacDonald the soles of his shoes would have gotten Briggs killed by some of the tribal warlords Mac had worked with in the Middle East, but here it was just part of the scenery.

"Nothing much to tell. The net is out and has been for months. No luck. Maybe the guy Monzo's people were hunting for just looks like Slate."

"You and I read the same report from the FBI, Mac. A dozen or more hard guys killed in two days and Monzo and his brother burned up in the Cricket. This was a pro hit. You saw the pictures from the van and the warehouse. Shell casings from automatic weapons all over the place, military grade ammo. We're talking a team of trained killers here, not a bunch of neighborhood goombahs."

Briggs took his feet down from the desk and leaned forward in the chair. "Turn around, Mac."

MacDonald turned in his chair and saw something he hadn't seen when he came in. On the back of the office door was a Xerox copy of the artist's sketch that had been circulated around Newark and The City. It showed a man with a mustache and dark hair over a scar that split his left eyebrow. Beside it was a dossier photo of Slate blown up to equal size. The resemblance was close enough.

"Every time I look up, I see that face to remind me Slate's still out there, and maybe others from his team. I don't need to tell you what damage he can do if says the right things to the wrong people. The folks who tell me what time to go to bed at night bark up my ass all day long about it, and that's why I'm barking up yours. Find him, Mac. Soon."

Briggs picked up a file and flipped it open. He studied a page for a moment then looked up and said, "You won't find Slate under my desk, Mac," then went back to reading. The meeting was over.

As MacDonald walked away from Briggs's office, he understood once again why the Company made them check their weapons at the door. Briggs was just a pencil pusher, some Senator's kid from the Diplomatic Corps who kissed enough asses and pulled enough strings to buy the desk he occupied now.

The words of a protest song he'd heard on the radio on the ride in echoed in his head: John Fogarty's raspy voice singing, "It ain't me. It ain't me. I ain't no senator's son, son. It ain't me. It ain't me. I ain't no fortunate one." The smug preppie had never been in the field, and beyond the standard self-defense training all personnel get, Briggs had no experience. Put him on the street in Saigon without his security escort and he'd be crying for his mama in five minutes.

Mac could break Briggs over his knee, and Briggs knew it, but he loved to poke a stick through the bars and remind Mac who was in charge. Mac would double his effort and probably still not find Slate unless he was damned lucky or some *deus ex machina* swooped down and swatted Slate for defying the gods. Mac was good, but there was good and then there was Slate and then there was the Devil, or maybe Mac had the last two backward.

X

"Somebody light a cigarette and toss it out here. I don't want to come inside," Swede yelled through the screen door. Slate lit one and strolled out onto the porch where Swede stood barefoot wearing only cut-off fatigue shorts and dripping swamp water on the rough boards. The black commas of leeches dotted his legs and abdomen.

"Bloodsucking bastards," he said. "I quit counting at sixteen."

"Like you quit spelling at fifteen?"

"Up yours, Haines. Give me that cigarette, Johnny." Slate passed the cigarette to Swede. He took a drag on it to heat up the tip and pressed it against the shiny back of a leech on his thigh. The leech twisted and let go, and Swede brushed it off. It fell to the porch and Swede brought his heel down on it.

"You don't really need a cigarette, Swede," Haines said. "Watch and learn." He slid a fingernail under a leech on Swede's forearm and pushed the sucking mouth away with his fingernail. As soon as it let go, Haines swept his finger backward under the leech's fat hind part and flicked it away. "See how easy?"

"It removes the payback component, though. More fun this way." Swede singed another leech. "So where are we going tonight?"

"We're sticking close to home. I don't want to run into any more hunters."

"We handled it okay last night," said Haines. "All we have to do is stay out of sight, and as I recall, that's something we know how to do."

Slate had another reason to run the pack near the camp. He wanted them to change in front of Singer to see how he'd react to having the three of them in his face when the moon came up. It was risky, but not as big a risk as going on an op and finding out the hard way if Singer snapped.

"Tonight, we keep it close to home. Almanac says moonrise is 18:39 hours, so don't take a trip to town for a cold one."

"Okay, Johnny," said Swede, crushing another leech underfoot. "Whatever you say."

XI

Jimmy hadn't called Roxy the day after the incident at the Knob. He was embarrassed at his cowardice, although most reasonable people would agree that not attacking three werewolves with a ball bat was the course of true wisdom. But Jake already mailed the picture of the track they found and a letter he wrote for Billy to sign with him telling the story embellished with a few extra details.

Whether he wanted to or not, he'd have to call Roxy to make sure she didn't tell anybody else about it or contradict his version of the story, especially the part he didn't tell Jake about, pissing his pants.

He spent the better part of the morning thinking about how to handle it and had a rehearsed script in his head. It was already two-thirty when Billy called but when Roxy came to the phone, she sounded half asleep.

"Hey, Rox."

"Oh, Billy. Hi." She didn't exactly sound glad to hear his voice.

"Uh, did I wake you up? I'm sorry."

"I haven't slept much since Friday night."

"Me either." Stick to the script.

"Maybe next time we could just go to a movie or get a pizza or something."

This was getting away from him. "Uh, yeah, sure. That'd be great. Listen, Roxy, you didn't tell anybody what we saw did you?"

"I haven't told anybody yet. Why?" An edge crept into her voice.

"Well, people will think we're wackos. And I'm kinda worried about the pot, you know? We might get into trouble."

"Or maybe the whole school will find out you went out with me. You didn't even ask how I am when I picked up the phone. All you're worried about is you. If you'd called me yesterday, I might have thought different, but it's too late, Billy."

Things were going downhill in a hurry. "No, Roxy, it's not like that I..."

"That's right: I, I, I. You wouldn't think that maybe I don't want the whole school to know I went out with a big dumb jock who pees his pants."

She hung up before Billy could think of something to say. He was afraid to call her back.

XII

Rather than trash the inside of the cabin, the team opted to be outside for the change. They were hunkered down in the hard-packed dirt in front of the porch having a last cigarette as the Georgia twilight deepened into darkness. Singer sat on the porch in a chair he'd dragged from the kitchen. His hands were empty, but Slate knew the automatic with its silver ammo was tucked under his shirt in the back of his jeans.

Tonight was crucial as far as Singer was concerned. If he could work with the others without letting his emotions interfere, then they'd be okay. If he couldn't, then Slate would have to make a hard decision, whether to risk turning him involuntarily before the moon set.

"What time's it getting to be, Singer?" Slate said around his cigarette.

"18:36 hours. Almost show time." He sounded nonchalant, but the pitch of his voice betrayed his anxiety.

The cry of a loon echoed over the water. Perfect, thought Slate. Lunacy from the word *Luna* for moon put the two together and you get loon. He looked to the porch and saw Singer sitting in the gloaming with his hands on his knees, but it was too dim to tell how hard he was squeezing them.

They had thoroughly scouted the peninsula where the camp was located and it was familiar ground. Tonight's run was strictly maneuvers, calculated to make the team work as a pack in their bestial form, to take advantage of the instincts and other advantages the werewolf form provided and synergize them with the team's training and experience.

Moonrise.

The change began and although Slate tried to keep an eye on Singer, he was soon distracted by the physical racking as his body shifted its shape. When the change was complete, Slate stood upright and turned to the cabin. His enhanced vision showed him the taut lines of Singer's face but also showed him Singer's hands still clenched on his knees. Slate's sensitive ears picked up Singer's measured breathing. He was keeping himself calm in the face of the horror, a point to the good.

Slate growled and gave the follow sign to Swede and Haines. He turned to Singer and gave him a thumbs-up. Singer nodded but didn't move his hands. Slate turned and set off running and the others followed him into the moonlit marsh.

Singer sat for a long time staring into the darkness. Okay, he watched it happen. Nobody got hurt. He kept his emotions in check, but they were still there. The team didn't threaten him in any way, but he still felt uneasy, the same as he would if he lived in a house with a pet tiger. Maybe it was domesticated and used to being around people, but there was always the risk that some unknown factor would trigger its feral instinct and the oversized house pet would take off his head with a swipe of its paw.

He'd fought side by side with these guys for years and he owed his life to every one of them from one fight or another. Leaving the team was the last thing he wanted to do, but if he couldn't bring himself to the point that he could sleep in the same room with them in wolf form, it wasn't going to work. He'd have to bail for everybody's good.

Slate signaled the team to separate. Each of them took a different path through the scattered pines intending to rendezvous at a prearranged point two miles away. The maneuver would test their ability to remember plans and orders given while they were human once they became werewolves. It would also test their ability to carry out individual roles in the team's mission.

The moonlight gave a ghostly cast to the Spanish moss that draped the pond cypress trees that rose from the swamp like pillars. The night sounds of crickets and frogs and an occasional owl came from a distance, but not nearby, as if nature held its breath while the monsters passed.

Slate's wolf vision made the moonlit landscape as bright as dawn. The blood pumped to his iron-hard muscles as he ran, long loping strides that covered twice the distance in half the time he could as a human. The air whistled past his ears as he tore down the path leaping fallen trees and patches of mire and pools of bog water. He felt freer than he ever had in his life.

The first rendezvous point was a half hour away at an old tin fishing shanty on a small finger of land that became an island when the rains were heavy. Haines was the first to arrive followed soon after by Slate.

They waited for Swede out of sight in the shack. Letting him run on his own would prove his control and his capability. Two minutes passed, then three and Slate was about to go looking for Swede when they heard his tread approaching.

Through the doorway, Slate saw Swede break from the shadows of the trees into the moonlight and cross the narrow spit of land to the shack. His breath steamed in the cool air as he trotted into the shanty.

"Okay?" growled Slate.

"Okay," said Haines in return.

Both looked to Swede, whose mouth moved but with no words, just a grunting snarl. He raised his thumb and nodded.

Slate held up two fingers then extended his right arm behind him and brought it forward. Move out.

The second rendezvous was a grove of pines halfway around the lake that required Haines and Slate to go one direction and Swede the other. The second run was much longer, nearly two hours, and all three arrived within a minute of one another like clockwork. Swede was doing well. One more turn and they'd go back to the camp to cool down before moonset.

As he ran, Slate marveled at the stamina the change provided. He had been running full tilt for hours and still felt as if he could go on forever. His dark form flashed from shadow to shadow among the trees, one with the night.

The third rendezvous point was a flat, open area dominated by a lone pine tree. The trunk was split by lightning years before, but the tree had persevered almost in defiance of the elements. Slate had scouted this site earlier and chose it because he found signs of animal activity; coarse bristles on the rough pine bark and the furrows of turned earth like scars in the soil: a feral boar. The spoor told Slate that although the boar was alone; its size would make it a formidable opponent, a worthy test for the pack.

They had hunted one a few weeks before for its meat, stalked it and killed it with rifles, but tonight, if the beast were there, they would face it with nothing more than their fangs, their claws, and their teamwork.

As he rounded a bend in the path, Slate could smell the harsh, musky scent of the boar nearby. As he broke into the clearing, he saw it near the tree. It weighed at least four hundred pounds, maybe more, covered in dark bristles that painted it a mottled gray and black. The boar's razor sharp tusks flashed white in the moonlight.

The boar was agitated and in a few seconds, Slate saw the reason. Swede was approaching from the east side of the clearing and the boar had seen him.

Unlike most animals that instinctively fled an unnatural intruder, the boar stood its ground, digging its hooves into the earth, throwing chunks of sod, and clashing its tusks together. Its bristles rose and fanned out, making it look larger than it was, an instinctive ploy to frighten away opponents. The animal grunted in an angry staccato rhythm. Swede strode closer, one cautious step at a time. The boar snorted a final warning and charged.

Swede was a diversion. As the boar rushed at him, a dark blur shot from the trees to the boar's left side: Haines. The ungainly boar tried to swivel in mid-charge to meet the new attacker, but it wasn't quick enough. Haines vaulted the boar's back and slashed with his claws, tearing furrows like a plowed field through the bristled hide. The boar squealed in pain and rage and wheeled, slashing its tusks at Haines and finding only air.

Swede ran in at the boar and raked his claws over its thick snout as the head swung back. One of the tusks caught Swede in the calf, a long gash that barely missed his Achilles' tendon. Swede countered with a blow of his hairy fist to its forehead that would have killed a lesser animal. The boar blinked and rocked backward then immediately resumed its attack, grunting in anger.

Because of the heavy bristles, thick skin, and dense layer of fat across its back, the slashes Haines made did little substantial harm although they bled profusely.

The scent of blood filled Slate's nostrils and he dove under the boar, digging his claws into its belly and ripping out a chunk of flesh. The thick girdle of muscle in the animal's abdomen kept Slate from hitting a vital organ but the pain was severe. The boar stomped its foot and grazed Slate's scalp, drawing blood.

The beast twisted from side to side slashing with its tusks, trying to defend itself in all directions at once. It swiveled, faster than Slate would have anticipated and got its snout under him as he tried to rise. It threw him into the air and Slate landed hard on his back.

The boar would have gored him with its tusks if Swede hadn't clamped his jaws on its hind leg, crushing the joint. Haines leapt onto the squealing animal's back and held it by one ear as he dragged his claws across its eyes. The hog rolled over and nearly pinned Haines under its weight, but Haines was too quick and jumped aside.

Blinded, the animal went into a panic, wheeling around the pivot of its good leg and tossing its head, slashing the empty air with its tusks. Slate held up a fist. Hold. The pack stood still. The boar stopped its mad whirling, confused by the sudden silence. Slate gestured to Haines, who shuffled backward a step. When the boar turned its head toward the sound, Swede dove in from its other side, clamping his jaws into the vulnerable flesh on the underside of its neck. Swede shook his head viciously from side to side and ripped open the boar's throat.

Hot blood jetted out as the boar made one last swipe of its head then fell over, its sides heaving. The pack stood around the kill and raised their heads to the moon and howled.

Slate turned to his brothers in arms and said, "Okay?"

Haines growled back, "Okay."

Swede struggled for a moment, growling out words like "aray" and "ogar" before finally forcing out, "Ogay."

Haines and Slate clapped Swede on the back.

Then the grisly communal feast began.

The pack ran back to the camp, exhilarated at the fight and the kill. Over his shoulder, Swede carried a haunch he'd ripped from the boar. They arrived back at the camp an hour before moonset.

Singer was waiting on the porch where they'd left him. He stiffened when he saw Swede coming toward him and his hand crept behind his back. Swede swung the bloody boar's haunch down and laid it on the porch beside Singer's chair and said in words barely understandable, "One for all; all for one."

Moonset.

By the time they changed, their superficial cuts and scratches were healed and the worst injuries, the gash in Swede's calf and the cut on Slate's scalp were well on their way. Pegg called it a "benefit" of the condition; the physical trauma of transformation being so disruptive that the affected body compensated by healing much more rapidly.

Slate's body ached from the fight with the boar and would hurt worse when he woke up later, but the night's adventure served its purpose. The team functioned as a unit, and the participatory kill bonded them. Swede proved he could be trusted, and at least for the moment, Singer seemed to be stable. One more night, a short one, and they could start planning. Slate had survived and he had escaped; now it was time for the third leg of the triangle: payback.

XIII

"Still think that wasn't a bear we saw the other night?" Jack Martin prodded with the toe of his boot at the half eaten carcass of the boar and swatted at the cloud of black flies that swarmed around it. "A gator, if he was big enough, would've dragged him back into the swamp and taken him to his nest under a bank someplace. He's way too torn up for a bobcat or a pack of dogs to have done it."

"And I suppose the bear tore the whole haunch off of that pig and took it with him for a snack later, huh?"

"Maybe some other hunters found him while the meat was fresh and took it. I say it's a bear and a big one. We need to set out some traps."

XIV

November 19, 1969
Manville, South Carolina

Maura Jameson watched the researcher with more than casual interest. Her profession as an anthropologist made her a people watcher as a matter of course, but the mystery man, as she came to think of him was a special case. He had come into the Manville University Library the last three days in a row and sat at the same seat at the same table, a back corner facing the door. She had to admit that she noticed him at first because he was good-looking in a rough sort of way and he seemed to be in good shape, something she found attractive in a man. She quickly found him intriguing for another reason: the books.

The dark-haired stranger would sit for hours taking notes as he pored over books whose titles she could read and recognize at a distance, books on the occult, pagan religions, mythology, and particularly lycanthropy, a subject she'd studied and written about extensively. As an anthropologist, Maura Jameson had spent most of her academic career pursuing subjects that her colleagues scoffed at, but she was never one to be deterred by peer pressure.

She was in the second month of a research sabbatical and spent more of her time in the university's cavernous library than anywhere else, gathering source material for a book on primitive tribal rituals and their analogs in medieval Europe. Maura believed as did Jung that shared subconscious threads from humanity's earliest days manifested themselves in the human psyche through all the ages, linking the most basic religious beliefs and practices, including ritual magic.

Today the stranger was sitting with a copy of Berger's *Man and Beast: The Psychology of the Other* and copying titles and authors from the book's bibliography. She would have dismissed him as just another graduate student working on a doctoral dissertation except for his hands. The stranger's hands were scarred, and some knuckles bulged where bones had been broken. These weren't the hands of an academic. The scar that split his eyebrow was only one of many small ones that mapped a hard life across his face.

Maura took a seat at a nearby table and went to work. The mystery man sat for nearly an hour copying titles from the back of Berger's text before he rose and strode to the card catalog. Maura noticed that any time he left his seat the mystery man took a file folder with his notes under his arm as if it were a cashier's check for a million dollars. Researchers were often very secretive, afraid that another scholar might steal their ideas and their glory, but the oddities about this man made her think otherwise.

She watched him cross from the card catalog to the circulation desk and let curiosity get the best of her. She scribbled a title on a slip of paper and followed him over. She came up beside him in time to hear the librarian tell him, "I'm sorry, sir, but that volume is in the rare books collection and is only available for use by faculty members." A quick glance at the slip on the counter showed her the title: Člŏvĕk a Vlk, *Human, and Wolf* by Egon Czarko.

The mystery man nodded and turned away without argument. Maura followed him a few steps and said, "Excuse me, sir?" He turned. "Maybe I can help you."

Slate had come into the Manville University Library; a hundred fifty miles away from the compound in search of information that could help him use the amulet to ease the transition from human to werewolf for himself and for his men. It was the third library he'd combed for information in as many weeks. The library was vast, and the sections on folklore, witchcraft, and magic gave him plenty of leads but nothing substantial. Too many of the sources either parroted general information or quoted each other, leading him in a long slow circle as he checked and cross-referenced book after book.

The Czarko book, although it was in the Czech's native language was said in the card catalog to be illustrated. It was a long shot, but it might have a picture of the amulet and if it did, translation of the Slovak text wasn't impossible.

Slate didn't protest when the woman at the desk denied his request. He didn't want to draw undue attention to himself. As he walked away, someone called to him. He recognized her as the woman who had been sitting two tables away. He'd seen her in the library before and took the same notice of her that he did of any stranger who entered his space. Now he appraised her more thoroughly.

She was tall and athletic, dark-haired and fair-skinned but with a ruddy cast that told of recent time spent outdoors. Her eyes were green, and her nose turned up a little. "How could you help me?" Slate said, eyeing her warily.

"I'm a faculty member, and I could call for the book on my ticket. If you like, you can examine it with me."

"I wouldn't want to be any bother," Slate said.

"It wouldn't be a bother at all. Actually, I'm familiar with the book. I studied it a few years ago." Slate stared at her. She put up her index finger. "Wait just one moment." She disappeared into the labyrinthine shelves and returned with a book in her hand. She held it up for Slate to see. *Lycanthropy through the Ages.* Before he could comment, she turned the book around to show him the back cover. Her picture was on the dust jacket.

The corners of her mouth turned upward. "As you can see, I'm very interested in the subject, and if I can help someone else mine the same topic, I'd be happy to oblige."

Slate thought it over and decided to take the offer. "All right, I could use the help, uh, Miss Jameson?"

"Please, call me Maura," she said, holding out her hand. Her grip was firm and her handshake confident. Her eyes betrayed no guile. "Jim," Slate said, "Jim Burns."

"It will take an hour or so to have the book available. Is that all right?"

"Sure."

"Do you read Slovak?"

"No, I don't."

"Well, you're in luck; I do."

He smiled. "The catalog said the book was illustrated. I was interested in seeing the pictures."

"Člověk a Vlk is from the late nineteenth century," Maura said. "Almost all of the engravings are taken from old woodcuts but they are fairly detailed. Is there something specific you're looking for?"

"I'll know it when I see it."

Maura nodded and smiled, half amused by his reticence. "We have some time, Jim, so why don't we go have a cup of coffee while we wait?"

• • •

Maura watched Slate's hands, the careful precision of his movements belying their coarse appearance as he set her cup on the Formica tabletop. "Would you like cream or sugar?"

"Neither." She said, chuckling. "I got in the habit of drinking it black from years spent in the middle of nowhere, places where cream and sugar were in short supply."

"Where was that?"

"The Brazilian rainforest, the northern tundra of Siberia, even the Heart of Darkness, the Belgian Congo."

"I drink mine black for pretty much the same reason, just different locations. Go on job sites, and any milk you find usually has tentacles growing out of the carton. As for sugar, who knows what some fool might have put in the bowl as a joke; sand, alum, plaster dust . . ."

"What kinds of job sites?"

"All sorts. Most recently I was a troubleshooter for Brown & Root in Viet Nam, military construction mostly." The story wasn't entirely true or false. The B&R job was cover for Slate and his team and gave them an excuse to be most of the places they were.

"And now you're here studying werewolves?"

Slate gave her a blank stare and Maura realized that her segue was a little too blunt. "I'm sorry, I shouldn't be so nosy. It's just that I find so few people interested in the same things I am that when I do I want to know all about it."

Slate smiled, relaxing a little. "I've been fascinated with the occult since I was a kid. I had some vacation time coming, so I decided to use it to do something that interests me for a change."

Maura nodded, thinking, that's okay, Jim Burns. If I had a hot research lead I wouldn't be too forthcoming to somebody I just met either. Let's just play this out and see where it goes.

XV

The library's rare book collection was housed in a back corner of the second floor. The walls were tinted glass panels set in steel frames. The whole room looked completely out of place amid the Gothic architecture of the rest of the building. Slate heard a pneumatic hiss when Maura opened the door. "The room is air tight and climate controlled to curb deterioration of the ink and paper," she said. "The lighting minimizes ultraviolet exposure."

As Slate followed Maura into the room, a small woman in a plaid pantsuit and white turtleneck waved them over to her desk. "Hello, Doctor Jameson," she said. "The book you requested is ready. Follow me, please." She led them into a windowless room with a table and chairs. On the table sat a slim book the size of a telephone directory bound in cracked green leather. A buckled strap held its covers closed.

"Betty will assist you."

A young woman in jeans and a sweater with her sandy hair pulled back into a ponytail smiled and nodded. "So that you both can see the book, I'll sit between you." She took her seat and pulled on a pair of white cotton gloves.

Slate gave Maura a quizzical look. "She's trained to turn the pages with minimal wear and damage."

"What pages would you like to see, Doctor Jameson?"

"Our interest is primarily in the illustrations, Betty, so if there is no list of them at the front of the book, we'll have to go page by page."

Betty began, slowly turning each page with a crackling of the old vellum. She looked to Maura each time, Maura nodded, and Betty turned the next page.

It was slow going, and after ten minutes Slate had to fight the impatient urge to grab the book from Betty's hands and flip through it with his thumb. The first few illustrations were as Maura said, engravings of old woodcuts, but their detail was sharp. They pictured different artists' renderings of werewolves, a few in stages of transformation, but most were portrayed in full monstrous form. The drawings were often crude and stylized but their impact was not diminished by that fact. These were portraits of terror.

By the time they had turned over a hundred pages Slate was getting a headache from staring at the pages of indecipherable script. Then Betty turned one more page and Slate saw it: the amulet.

The picture was an engraving but not a copy of a woodcut. The detail was exact, and Slate recognized some of the runes that decorated the twisted vines of silver. "Stop."

Maura and Betty looked up in surprise. Slate had sat silent since she began turning the pages. "This is what you were looking for?" Maura said hesitantly.

"Yes."

Maura bit her lip and nodded slowly. "Do you know what this is?"

"That's what I'm here to find out."

"That is a *farkas ostor*; literally translated from Bulgarian it means 'wolf whip.'"

"What does the text on the page say?"

"Betty, turn back one page, please." Maura read the Slovak text and gave a loose translation. "It tells the story of the attack of the Bulgarian city of Cherven by a pack of ravenous wolves driven from the mountains by an unusually severe winter in 1427. The wolves were so numerous and so savage that the people fled into the citadel for protection. Spring came but the wolves did not retreat. The people of Cherven were held prisoner in the fortress by them. The food ran out and some reverted to eating the dead.

"It was then that the lords of the city took a drastic measure." Maura looked up. "Betty, turn the page, please." She went on, "In the citadel's keep was a man named Janos Bok, imprisoned for life as a sorcerer. The lords offered him a pardon if he could rid the city of the scourge. Bok called for silver, particularly the crucifixes that hung from rosaries, melted them down and forged the amulet called the *farkas ostor.*

"Bok ordered the citadel gates be opened and he strode out to meet the snarling pack. He held the *farkas ostor* before him and mouthed words no one could hear. As one, the wolves ceased howling and snapping and

"What pages would you like to see, Doctor Jameson?"

lay down on the sward. He put his hand in the mouth of the pack's leader and drew it away unbitten. Then he mouthed a command and all the wolves ran away from the fortress and over a cliff into the river where they drowned, like the demon possessed swine of the New Testament. The story grew that the *farkas ostor* could control even the *vŭrkolatsi* – werewolves.

"The legend has it that the *farkas ostor* was buried in Bok's tomb in the Cherven necropolis, and to this day, no wolf has ever been seen in the city."

"Does the account tell how the *farkas ostor* was used? What spells or rituals made it work?"

"Betty, turn the page, please. Again." Maura looked up. "There is no more about it in this text, but I know of one book where that may be found. But first, tell me why you want to know?"

Slate's eyes shifted to Betty. Maura said to her, "I think we're done here, Betty. Thank you. You can return the book now." Betty nodded and carefully closed the book, buckled the closure strap and carried it out of the room, closing the door behind her.

"We're alone now. Whatever you tell me I will hold in the strictest confidence. Before we take this any further, I have to know why you're seeking this knowledge."

Slate stood with a jerk, shoving his chair back from the table. He turned toward the door.

"Wait." Maura reached to grab his sleeve and knocked the folder from his hand. It fell to the floor and papers and notes fanned out across the carpet, Maura's eye fell on the image of the *farkas ostor*. Before Slate could scoop it up, Maura snatched it from the floor and stared at it as her mouth slowly opened and closed again. "My God," she whispered. "That's not a drawing; it's a rubbing." She stared at Slate. "You have a *farkas ostor*?"

Sometimes decisions are made for you. Slate hesitated then nodded and said gravely, "Yes, and it's a matter of life and death that I learn how to use it."

Slate wasn't comfortable revealing anything to Maura Jameson, but the next full moon was less than a week away, and she had knowledge that he needed. He hadn't given her his real name, and Manville University was four hours away in another state, so it wasn't likely she would show up uninvited at his front door if he decided she couldn't be trusted. The more she knew about Slate's situation, the more danger she would face, but he trusted his gut and decided to take her into his confidence just far enough to learn about the amulet, the *farkas ostor*.

"The book that you said had the rituals and spells, is it here?"

"No, but I know where there is a copy."

"Where is that?"

She met his eyes with an uncompromising stare. "*Quid pro quo*, Jim. Where did you find a *farkas ostor*?"

Slate smiled. "New Jersey."

"New Jersey."

"You asked where I found it. I found it in new Jersey."

"O-kay," she said slowly. "And where is it now?"

"In a safe place."

Maura took a deep breath and let it out. "I sincerely hope so."

XVI

Swede heard the crack of a rifle two hundred yards away and left his blind to investigate. He'd been waiting out a herd of deer that frequently crossed a spit of hard ground at the edge of the swamp in the hope of shooting fresh meat for dinner. He was wearing a ghillie suit that covered him to his feet and carrying an M-16. Haines had joked with him about it, using an automatic combat weapon to hunt deer. "What are you going to do? Make the whole species extinct?"

"It's set on single shot," Swede quipped back, "just to give the deer a sporting chance."

"Maybe it'd be more sporting if you hid in a tree with a Bowie knife and dropped on some big buck when he passed under it. See who wins then."

"Maybe next time. Right now, we're out of meat."

Swede threaded silently through the tangled brush and found a trail that led in the direction of the gunfire. He paralleled it through the undergrowth to avoid meeting someone coming the other direction. Ahead he heard voices. Swede set his weapon to full auto. He crept up on a clearing to see two men bending over a dead deer caught in a heavy-jawed trap.

The taller man wore a down vest, canvas hunting pants, and an Atlanta Braves ball cap. His companion was shorter and broader, dressed in a dun canvas jacket and jeans. Both wore green rubber boots. Swede was close enough to recognize the rifles propped against a nearby tree: a Mauser 30.06 and a Ruger M77, both with scopes.

They were so absorbed in getting the deer out of the trap that Swede could have crept up behind them and tapped them on the shoulder, or just shot both before they even knew he was there. He stood still to wait and watch.

"What do you want to do, Jack?" the shorter one said.

The tall one shrugged. I say we take the back straps and tenderloins and leave the rest as bait, reset the trap. The scent of a fresh kill ought to attract the bear."

Connor stood up and looked around as if he expected the bear to be sneaking up on them as they spoke. "Yeah, that sounds like the right idea." His gaze passed right over Swede crouched in the trees and Connor didn't see him in his camo. Let's reset the trap and get out of here before the damned bear does show up."

Swede slipped quietly away. These two were likely the poachers who took a shot at him two weeks before, and he was tempted to teach them a lesson, but the need to stay low overrode his personal feelings and he trotted back the way he came.

He'd have to tell John and the others about the trap. If they set one, they probably set others. One more thing to watch out for when they turned. Swede turned back toward the clearing. If he shadowed them, he could see where they set the other traps and come back later to spring them. The rednecks didn't have a dog with them; it would be easy. He just had to stay out of sight, something he knew all too well how to do.

XVII

"Hannisford," Paul Blaylock called through the open office door. "Get in here." Blaylock was *Unidentified*'s editor-in-chief and Bill Hannisford's primary pain in the ass. Hannisford hoped when he made the cover of *The Arcane Observer* with his werewolf pic earlier that year he was on his way to fame and fortune, but his career path turned out to be just one more of life's disappointments.

The Arcane Observer paid him for the picture and never called him again. He thought they'd reward him with some plum assignments or maybe a full-time staff job, but they didn't even return his calls. The cash the mob guys gave him for taking them to the Pine Barrens where he got the shot evaporated quickly once he paid off his bookie and took care of three months' back rent, so when the job at *Unidentified* opened up, he grabbed it.

Hannisford's job was what the *Unidentified's* staff called working the "Yahoo squad." He followed up on the kook letters that poured into the magazine daily, reports of every kind of paranormal activity. *Unidentified's* offices were in Manhattan, but the pay was lousy, so he still lived in his crummy apartment across the river in Jersey and had to ride the train in every day because it cost too much to park his beat up Jeep.

Blaylock sat behind a table instead of a desk. It was littered with layers of photographs, manuscripts, and galleys. He was kicked back in his chair bouncing a tennis ball off the wall when Hannisford came in. "For God's sake, Hannisford, go on a diet. You weigh five pounds more every time I see you." Blaylock, a fitness fanatic, was as lean as a willow branch and never failed to remind everyone of the fact.

Hannisford dropped his bulk into a convenient chair. "What's up, boss?"

"Got a real gem for you to check out, Billy boy. Way down yonder in Georgia." He threw an envelope across the table. In it were five Polaroid snapshots of what looked like an animal track. The foot was five-toed with an angular pad at the ball and claw marks at the ends of the toes. "So whaddya think? Is it a fake?"

"Can't tell from these pics. Georgia, you said?"

Blaylock nodded. "Yep, a little burg called Chambliss. Those Polaroids came in a letter that told a story of not one but three werewolves. And here's the kicker: we got a second letter a day or two later from somebody else corroborating the story. So, since you're the resident werewolf expert, I'm sending you to Chambliss to check it out."

"Too bad they didn't see them in Paris." Hannisford's blasé tone masked his excitement. He'd seen tracks like these one time before, in the Jersey Pine Barrens. He stood heavily and stretched, yawning. "I'll go pack my gear. What's the deadline?"

"Eleven days if we're going to make the next issue. Hop to it."

Back at his apartment, Hannisford picked up his phone and dialed a number. After three rings, he heard a click then a gruff voice. "This is Elroy Poston. Leave a message."

Hannisford and Poston had struck up a relationship that neither would call more than a mutual benefit at the time of the trial. The Ranger didn't like Hannisford much, and the feeling was mutual, but both had seen a werewolf, Poston with his eyes and Hannisford with his camera, and if either were to see it again, their best bet was working together.

"Poston, this is Hannisford. We've got a lead. Call me back right away."

XVIII

"You don't talk much, do you, Jim?" Slate drove and Maura rode beside him. They were rolling up Interstate 95 headed to Durham, North Carolina.

"You're doing fine," Slate said. "The stories are interesting."

"I've just been rambling on and on. Your turn. Tell me about Viet Nam."

Slate didn't speak right away. "I was a field superintendent for Brown & Root. We were under contract with the Navy to build bases, hospitals, munitions depots and airfields. It was the first time the Navy ever contracted with a private company on so large a scale to build things usually done by the Seabees.

"I don't know what your politics are concerning the war, although I guess technically, it's undeclared so it's still a 'conflict.' I suppose I should ask before I go on, what's your position?"

"I didn't like the idea of getting involved over there, but now that we're in it, I think we should fight it to win once and for all. If we don't, we'll be back in ten years or someone else will pick up the ball like we did from the French and the world will be no better for it."

"That's a better attitude than average," Slate said. "You know what the anti-war protesters called Brown & Root? 'Burn and Loot.' Sure, there was theft of equipment and supplies, and there was graft but really not much worse than most job sites stateside. Part of my job was 'loss prevention,' and I guess I did it well enough."

"But you got out."

"I just had enough for a while. I could go back tomorrow if I wanted to, or next year, or never. There's always work around."

"Loss prevention sounds like cops and robbers."

"In some ways, yeah. I busted the bad guys. Trouble is, for every one of them I took off the board, two more stepped up to take his place. Let's just say the pay was good but the work was less than rewarding. I guess what bothered me most was that after it's all over, those people's lives won't be much different no matter who wins. They'll still be scratching the ground with a stick to grow enough food for today. Poor is poor, and those were the poorest people I've ever seen."

Maura watched Slate's face carefully. She was trained to read people, and her instincts told her that Jim Burns was handing her a line. Don't press too hard, she thought, just give it time and it'll all come out.

They were almost at Durham, North Carolina where an untitled journal lay in the archives of Duke University's library. Maura described it as a grimoire, a book of spells and incantations that had belonged to a self-styled wizard named Claude Devereaux who died in 1923. It was there they would find the key to unlock the secrets of the *farkas ostor*. What she didn't tell Burns was that although the journal was written in French, for secrecy's sake it was also written in code and that even she would have difficulty translating it.

To do so would require a special person, and Maura hoped that she could convince him to help them.

XIX

"Hey, Billy," Billy was putting his jacket in his locker when he saw Jake running up the hall of Chambliss High School waving a piece of paper. "Check it out, man. We're in."

"In what?"

"*Unidentified.* They wrote me back to confirm that we sent the picture. They want to run it, and get this, man: they're sending a reporter to talk to us and a photographer."

Billy hesitated. "Uh, look, Jake, I'm good with getting the hundred bucks, but I don't know about being interviewed for the magazine. I told my dad I was going to the movies with a couple of my friends. If he finds out I took his car to the Knob, he'll flip out." He also didn't want the whole world to know he was out on a date with Roxy, and if a magazine interviewed him, her name was sure to turn up.

Jake ignored him. "Man there's some real bucks to be made on this one, Billy. Maybe we'll be on the cover." He rambled on, but Billy didn't pay attention. He was staring up the hallway at Roxy. She stared back for a few seconds then turned with a flip of her head and the cuffs of her bell bottoms followed her legs around the corner and out of sight.

Curt Balzer and Ed Simmons found Elroy Poston hiking on one of the side trails that wound through Sector Six of the Pine Barrens. He was dressed in field greens and had a boonie hat cocked on his head. A rifle was slung over his shoulder and a .45 automatic rode his hip in a holster.

Balzer and Simmons wore the khaki and green uniforms of New Jersey State Game Wardens, the same as the one Poston had worn a few months before. Since his termination Poston had haunted the forest day and night armed, and in Barnett's opinion, unstable. Besides the potential danger, Poston posed there was always the possibility that friends of the mobsters he killed months before might come looking for him and pick up the gunfight where it left off.

Simmons and Balzer were no strangers to Poston. He had worked side by side with them for three years after he furloughed out of the Army Rangers. Barnett was right to send both of us to head him off, thought Balzer. Elroy could be a handful.

Balzer raised his hand in greeting and Poston stopped twenty feet away, effectively out of reach. The men eyed each other for a moment then Balzer broke the silence. "I'm sorry, Elroy, but we have orders to tell you to leave."

"Orders from who?"

"You know who, Elroy: Barnett. He says to tell you you're to leave and not come back."

"Ask him why he won't come out here and tell me himself. This is public land. I have every right to be here," said Poston, tapping the blue hunting license pinned to his chest in its plastic cover. "It's small game season."

Simmons jumped in. "And you're hunting rabbits with a 30.06 and a .45 automatic?"

"I paid my fees."

"That's not the issue, Elroy, and we all know it."

"Look, Elroy," said Balzer, "I know you got a raw deal on your job, and

I sympathize with you, but you can't keep coming out here every day with a gun on your hip."

"Barnett thinks I'm crazy, doesn't he?" Poston said in a cold, level voice. Balzer and Simmons didn't respond. "Well, boys, I don't have anything against either of you, and I don't want to put you in the middle, but I will tell you this: I'll be back tomorrow and the next day and the next day. I've been above board with you so far, but from now on I'll just make sure you don't see me."

Before either Balzer or Simmons could speak, Poston turned and strode into the thick brush. In two seconds he was invisible.

"What do we tell Barnett?" Simmons said.

"That we found Elroy, we told him to leave, and he left."

"That's a little bit shy of the whole picture, ain't it?"

"We're law enforcement officers. We ordered him to leave. If he comes back, we call the State Police and have him arrested for defiant trespass. Let them deal with him. We know his truck. We see it parked on site, and we tell Barnett. He can call it in. Personally, I'd rather not face off with Elroy again."

Simmons turned full circle peering into the forest and seeing only trees and brush. "That makes two of us."

XXI

Tom MacDonald threw the file onto his cluttered desk and picked up his cup of coffee, gone cold while he was reading. Everything was coming up zeroes, and he was convinced that if John Slate was alive, he wasn't in New Jersey. MacDonald and his men had sweated the few of Monzo's crew who survived what the FBI had nicknamed "The Jersey Purge" with no success. The most he got out of them was that they'd been given a sketch of a guy Monzo wanted found. Nobody knew who the guy was or why Monzo wanted him, so the lead died there.

He stared across the office to the cork board on the opposing wall. Headshots, most of them blurred from enlargement were pinned to it, Slate and the five members of his team.

Two of the faces had red Xs over them, Faro Douglas and Tyler Hitchcock, confirmed dead in Laos.

The Jersey field office deputy Ray Gargon walked in holding a sandwich and chewing a bite of it. "No word on the Lost Boys, Mac." He studied the photos. "Are they really the badasses everybody says they are?"

MacDonald stared into his cup. "Usually, when we send a team on some black op, each member has a specialty; communications, demolition, interrogation, whatever. There are no specialists in this bunch. Any one of them can handle anything and if need be, pull off the op singlehanded if the others buy it." He looked up to emphasize his point. "Think of them as Renaissance men of death and destruction."

"The Company thinks Slate's alive and in country; what about the others?"

"That's the hell of it, Ray. We have no way of knowing, maybe 'til it's too late."

"What do you mean, Tom?"

"You never train people with the thought that they may turn on you someday. Maybe we trained these guys too well and they'll come back and bite us."

XXII

"I thought we were going to Duke University," said Slate looking over his shoulder at the stately towers and spires looming over the mundane architecture a few blocks away.

Maura smiled. "Did I say Duke University? I thought I said, Durham. The man we're going to see isn't associated with Duke; not anymore."

"Are you going to tell me his name?"

"He'll introduce himself to you when you meet, that is if he trusts you."

"Trusts me?"

"You have to understand the academic personality, Jim. People like him devote a lifetime to research and inquiry. They are very guarded about what they know and where they found it. Someone is always waiting in the shadows to steal their research and grab the academic glory for themselves."

"That isn't why I'm here."

"So you say, but up to now, you've asked for everything and volunteered nothing. We just met, and I don't really know you at all. You apparently have access to a rare, powerful, and dangerous artifact and all you'll tell me about it is that you found it in New Jersey.

Slate stared unspeaking through the windshield and Maura went on. "You'll understand if I have a few questions. For me to help you learn to use a *farkas ostor* is like me giving you bullets for an empty gun. Also, I have a solid working relationship with this gentleman and I don't want to jeopardize that. He's a fountain of information, but he's very guarded about who he shares it with."

"But he was associated with Duke at one time?" Slate knew Duke's thirty-year reputation as an institution for paranormal research.

"Yes, but no longer. His colleagues and the University felt his research methods were a little too extreme for an established institution. He resigned under a cloud six years ago and hasn't been back since."

Duke faculty, paranormal researcher, resigned in 1963, living in Durham, should be easy enough to find him whether he agrees to see me or not, Slate thought. Sit back and enjoy the drive.

Maura pointed. "Pull over there." Slate parked the van beside a telephone booth. "Wait here. I'm going to call to see if he'll agree to see you." She strolled to the booth and pulled the door closed behind her. While she fished in her pocket for a dime, Slate pulled a thin 10X scope from his jacket.

Maura dropped the dime in the coin slot and dialed the number. All of the digits were easy to spot through the glass side of the booth except the second one, but it was part of the phone exchange; the nine in the last four digits confirmed what Slate suspected, a pay phone.

The conversation lasted a few minutes and Maura came back to the van with a noncommittal expression. She opened the door and slid into the seat. "He's agreed to meet with us in two hours."

Slate nodded.

"In the meantime, we need to find some lunch. My stomach is starting to digest itself. Do you like fried chicken? There's a great diner a couple of blocks from here."

Slate followed Maura's directions and pulled into the parking lot of Mae's, a cinderblock building with striped red and white awnings shading the windows. He backed the van into a space in the macadam lot, all but putting his back bumper against the adjacent building.

"Angling for a quick getaway?" Maura joked, but not really.

"Old habit," Slate said. "Easier to pull out than back out if things get crowded." What he really wanted was to shield the license plate from easy view. He stole the plate from an almost identical van a week before and just in case, he had another taped under the driver's seat. Old habits.

The diner was vintage 50s, tricked out in Naugahyde booths with Formica tabletops and jukebox stations with flip pages connected to a big neon Wurlitzer that stood in all its glory at the far end of a black and white checkerboard floor. Twelve pedestal stools lined the counter and the smell of fry cooking was strong and inviting.

Two of the eight booths and three of the stools were occupied. Maura was ready to sit at a booth near the door but Slate ambled toward the back. He dropped into a seat facing the entrance. She was about to say something but thought better of it and sat opposite him.

A waitress in a white rayon uniform and a snood over her hair brought menus. Slate didn't open his. "You've been here before; what do you recommend?"

"The fried chicken, of course. You'd be surprised how much you miss it when you go to somebody else's country. They don't have a clue. Order the dinner special, half a chicken, mashed potatoes, and corn. You won't be sorry."

Slate smiled at her enthusiasm. "Sold."

The waitress took their order and while they waited, Slate flipped through the music selections. He dropped a quarter in the slot and punched in some numbers. The jukebox came alive with Wilson Picket's "In the Midnight Hour."

"That's another thing you miss out-of-country," he said. "American Pop music. We could get Armed Forces Radio from Saigon, but they didn't play the edgier stuff. I didn't hear much Stax or Atco while I was there."

"I appreciate the sentiment," Maura said. "You don't hear much of it in the Amazon jungle either. One thing I've always appreciated about American radio is the diversity. Where else can you turn on the radio and in the same half hour hear The Beatles, Frank Sinatra, James Brown, The Iron Butterfly, Henry Mancini and Patsy Cline all on the same station?"

Slate nodded. A man had come in since they ordered their food. He was late forties, maybe early fifties, his shoulder-length dark hair shot with gray, no beard but unshaven. He wore wraparound sunglasses and a green T-shirt with a peace sign emblazoned in yellow. Faded Levis and sandals finished off his outfit.

The chicken arrived and it was everything Maura said it would be. Halfway through his meal, Slate saw the man at the counter was still on his first cup of coffee. He hadn't changed position in almost a half hour, angled slightly giving him a good view of Slate and Maura in the mirror across the counter.

"Why don't you ask your friend to join us?"

Maura blinked. "What?"

"The old hippie at the counter in the peace shirt. That's him isn't it?"

"Uh . . ."

"You called him from the phone booth, but he didn't tell you two hours. He said, 'come to the diner and I'll check the guy out.' Right?"

Maura bit her lip. Her face reddened. "Was it that obvious?"

"You might as well invite him over. If he says yes, good. If he says no, I won't waste any more time waiting for him."

Maura shook her head. "Okay, you got me. I'll go ask him to come over." She slid out of the booth and walked down the counter to the syncopated strains of Sam and Dave's "Hold on, I'm Comin'." She sat beside the hippie and they put their heads together for a moment. He nodded and the pair came to the booth as Aretha Franklin launched into Otis Redding's "Respect."

Slate sat motionless, both hands flat on the table, face neutral as Maura slid to the inside of the booth and her friend took off his sunglasses and sat opposite him. He mirrored Slate's posture and manner. Non-adversarial but cautious. Without the glasses, his eyes were a pair of black gimlets.

"Professor, this is Jim Burns."

"No it isn't," said the Professor. "His name is John Slate and he is a werewolf."

Maura's mouth fell open. Slate's face didn't twitch. "Where did you get an idea like that, Professor?"

"We have—I should say had—an acquaintance in common: Derek Pegg."

Pegg. The wizard Monzo co-opted to control Slate and Joey Cimino as werewolves using the amulet, the *farkas ostor*.

"I understand Pegg was shot to death a few months ago. Is that not correct?" The Professor's voice was unnerving in its calm matter of fact delivery as if he were reading a grocery list aloud.

"It is." Drop the pretense, thought Slate. If he knows this much, he probably knows a lot more. Let's find out how much. "I can say with a straight face that I didn't shoot him."

"Then who did?"

"One of Michael Monzo's gunmen who also died during the shootout at his headquarters in Newark." Slate stopped short of saying that on his orders Pegg was drugged and strapped to the passenger seat of the van that he and his team used to get into the old factory site where the racketeer ran his drug ring; Pegg was collateral damage in the bloody gunfight that followed.

"Pegg was a brilliant man and a good friend. How do I know you didn't kill him and I shouldn't hand you over to his followers?"

The jukebox suddenly ran out of music.

Maura looked from one man to the other and realized that she didn't really know the Professor any better than she knew Jim Burns, or John Slate, or whatever his name was. "Look," she said, "guys, this is a little too deep for me, so just let me out and . . ." Both men turned their eyes toward her and the unspoken imperative was clear: Stay put.

She took a deep breath, nodded once and said, "Okay, but for the record, this is more than I signed up for."

XXIII

The tires of Bill Hannisford's Jeep sang on the pavement as he and Elroy Poston rolled south on the Interstate, almost drowned out by the blaring rock'n'roll on the radio. Whatever happened to the music I knew when I was a kid, Poston thought. He looked over at Hannisford behind the wheel and snorted in disgust. The photographer's short sleeved safari shirt strained its buttons. The fat slob had one hand on the steering wheel and the other wrapped around his third Big Mac from the bagful they'd bought at a McDonald's. No wonder he's as big as a walrus, thought Poston. The difference between Hannisford and himself was the difference between living to eat and eating to live.

Hannisford was a puke, no doubt about it, but to Poston, he represented maybe the best chance to vindicate himself. His message came at just the right time. Barnett's men would keep Poston out of the Pine Barrens, but he was convinced that the werewolf he saw that night a few months ago was long gone anyway. Working for that idiotic magazine, Hannisford was a source for tips and leads, like the one they were pursuing now, and an expense account to pick up the tab.

Poston had seen a real live werewolf. He was sure of that, and from what Hannisford told him, the hitters from the Jersey mob seemed to think it was real too. He was determined to prove, if only to himself, that he wasn't crazy, and he was prepared to do whatever it took to make that happen, even putting up with a jerk like Hannisford.

Hannisford finished his sandwich and stuffed the wrapper in the bag. He didn't take out his hand until it was full of French fries. Poston shut his eyes and pulled his Ranger cap over them. Eight more hours.

Four cars behind them, the gray Ford kept pace, as if an invisible string joined the two. Mackenna and Shultz, FBI agents, had been tailing the Jeep since it entered Virginia.   Hannisford and Poston, a twofer, thought Mackenna. The Bureau was convinced that the two were linked to a bigger criminal conspiracy, and Poston and Hannisford traveling together reinforced that belief. In North Carolina, (added comma) they'd hand the tail off to another team and go home. In the meantime, follow and watch.

XXIV

Swede pushed aside the mound of rotting fish guts and teased the trigger on the bear trap with a three-inch tree branch. It snapped shut, tearing the bark and gouging the wood. That was the fourth trap he'd sprung from the five the local boys set for what they thought was a bear but was really a werewolf. He would have thrown the damned things into the swamp to send the yahoos a message, but each was chained to a tree with a heavy padlock. Next time, Swede thought, I'll bring bolt cutters. Either that or wait for the full moon and pull the tree out of the ground.

The swamp was a dangerous place, full of natural perils and a few human ones as well, but Swede felt right at home, being as dangerous armed or otherwise as anything the place had to offer. One more trap and he could go back to the camp, fire up the airboat and make a run to Red's, the glorified fishing shack at the north end of the swamp. Swede had developed a taste for Colt .45 Malt liquor since they'd come back stateside, and the thought of a couple of those washing down a po' boy sandwich made his mouth water.

Swede crossed a patch with swamp grass poking through the surface of shallow water that gave the illusion that the blades were growing through mirrored glass. He saw the traces of a cottonmouth swimming nearby, the chevron ripples trailing from his head, and stood still until it was a good distance away. Live and let live, he thought. The sun would set soon, and he wanted to finish dealing with the traps and get back before dark.

The fifth trap was chained to the roots of a cypress tree draped with a curtain of Spanish moss. The trap and the chain had been daubed with mud and if Swede hadn't already known where it was, he might have stepped in it himself. He picked up a tree branch that stuck out of the water and pushed it against the plate. The jaws of the trap snapped on it, biting deep into the branch.

Swede turned to walk away and heard the snap of a twig behind him. He reached for his automatic, but before it cleared the holster, a rifle cracked and Swede went down.

The wound wasn't lethal, but it was bad enough. Swede's right arm felt paralyzed; his fingers were numb. His automatic had fallen from the holster when he went down. The pistol lay under him and he couldn't reach it with his other hand. He kept his eyes shut as he heard footsteps creeping closer, then voices.

"Why the hell did you do that?" Connor said angrily. "Is he dead?"

"I don't know," Jack Martin said. "I saw him springing our trap and just saw red, that's all. Besides, he was reaching for a gun. You saw it. It was self-defense."

"Yeah? Try proving that to the Georgia Patrol with a hole going in his back and out his front. You dumbass. Now we're in some real trouble."

"Only if they find him."

Connor blinked. "What?"

"I say we throw him in the water whether he's dead or alive and let the gators have him. No body, no evidence, no crime."

Swede opened his eye a crack and saw two sets of rubber boots and two rifles leaning against the tree.

"Help me pick him up."

Connor took Swede's feet and Jack grabbed the shoulders of his jacket. "Damn," said Connor. "He's a big sumbitch. He weighs a ton. We'll have to drag him."

It hurt like hell but Swede gritted his teeth and made no sound as they pulled him roughly over the gnarled roots.

"Lots of blood. That's good," said Martin. "That'll bring the gators running. Take him over there." Martin gestured with a wag of his head.

Swede's left arm slipped under his jacket and his fingers closed on the handle of his Ka-Bar. He barely opened his eyelid and found his target, just behind Jack's beard.

Martin leaned over Swede to get a better grip. "Okay, Connor, let's

...a rifle cracked and Swede went down.

dump him right…" Martin's sentence and the thought behind it were interrupted by the tip of Swede's knife piercing him under his jaw, bursting through his tongue, and shoving through the roof of his mouth. A sharp twist of Swede's hand and the knife came free, slashing Martin's windpipe and jugular.

Swede's legs kicked out and caught the gaping Connor full in the chest, sending him sprawling backward into the water. The pain in his shoulder was red, but Swede's anger was crimson. He dragged himself to his feet and plunged into the marsh.

Connor floundered, trying to get a footing in the thick silt under the shallow water. "Hey. Mister," he babbled, "I didn't shoot you, Jack did. I won't tell. Honest." He tried to sit up and Swede brought the pommel of the knife down on the top of Connor's skull with the wet crunch of breaking bone. The redneck's eyes rolled back and he toppled into the water.

Swede put a foot on his chest to hold him under. Connor never struggled. A few bubbles and it was over.

He staggered to the edge of the water and sat heavily. Got to get up, he thought. His knife fell with a splash into the water and immediately sunk into the muck underneath. Got to keep moving. Can't pass out. Swede lurched to his feet and crossed to the tree where he'd sprung the trap. He threw the rifles into the muck with his good arm then picked up his automatic where it had fallen and started back toward camp as the shadows deepened in the swamp.

Haines sat on the porch of the cabin listening to what he called the changing of the guard, the sounds of the swamp's daytime wildlife yielding to the completely different sounds of its nocturnal creatures. The sky that showed through the trees was deepening from violet to black and a spray of stars showed through the pine trees.

The screen door groaned and Singer came out with a can of Budweiser in each hand. He set one beside Haines and popped the tab one-handed on his own. "Night sounds different every place you go."

Haines nodded. "Yep." He opened his can and took a long pull. "If Swede isn't back in five minutes, we'll go to Red's without him. We're about out of beer."

"Maybe we oughta go look for him."

"Would we need to look for you? Or for me?" Haines said. Singer shook his head. "There aren't three things in this swamp put together that are tougher than Swede. If he's not back, he has a reason."

Singer nodded and stood up. "You're right. I'll get the keys to the airboat." He was almost to the door when he caught a sound that didn't belong to the night, three gunshots two seconds apart. Singer dashed into the cabin and came back with a pistol in one hand and a flashlight in the other. Haines was already on his feet.

They stood in the yard and listened. Crickets, frogs, and whippoorwills. Singer pointed his automatic at the sky and fired three shots, a response to the distress signal. In a few seconds, three shots sounded nearby. "Ten o'clock," said Haines leading the way with the light. "Come on."

A hundred yards into the swamp they found Swede, back against a cypress trunk. The right side of his jacket was red with blood. His eyes were closed, but they could hear the ragged gasps of his breath.

"Let's get him back to the cabin." Haines heaved Swede to his feet and the big man groaned. He got Swede's good arm around his shoulders and half-walked half-dragged him back to the camp.

"Get the medical kit," barked Haines as Singer ran across the porch. Inside, he sat Swede on a kitchen chair. He pulled off his belt and threaded it through the chair back, under Swede's good arm and over his shoulder to keep him from falling forward.

Haines put a finger on Swede's neck. "Pulse is good." He flicked open his Buck knife and cut away Swede's jacket and the T-shirt underneath. "Bullet went through him back to front. The blood's just seeping right now." He felt the clavicle and the humerus. "Nothing broken that I can tell."

Singer handed Haines a rag and a bottle of peroxide. Haines put a flat lumber pencil between Swede's teeth. "Bite down." He poured peroxide over the raw exit wound and Swede's body stiffened as he grunted in pain.

"He's hurting pretty bad," said Singer. "Maybe we should shoot him up with morphine."

"Not yet. I don't know how much blood he's lost, and the dope could do him in if we slow his heart too much." Haines swabbed at the wound with a gauze pad. "I've got this. Check the perimeter and make sure whoever shot him isn't out there aiming through the windows."

In seconds Singer was out the door with a cut-down shotgun in his hands.

Haines dug in the medical kit and found a tennis ball-sized bulb syringe. He filed it with peroxide and aimed the nozzle into the hole in Swede's chest.

"Hold on, buddy. I have to flush the wound. This is gonna smart a little."

Haines squeezed the bulb and the disinfectant shot into the raw hole.

Swede jerked against the belt and his teeth dug into the wood of the pencil. Haines flushed the wound from the other side and stood back. Nothing to do now but wait and watch for trouble. He considered moving Swede but decided to leave him as he was rather than risk starting the bleeding again. There would be time to stitch him later after he was sure there was no residue in the tissue.

He took the pencil from Swede's teeth. "You're gonna be okay, buddy. No sweat."

"Too bad the moon ain't full." Swede looked up, his eyes bleary and trying to focus. "I lost my Ka-Bar, Mikey."

"Don't worry, man. We'll find it for you later. Look at me, Swede. How many were there?"

Swede raised his left hand. Two fingers.

"Still walking?"

Swede shook his head.

Haines picked up the rags of Swede's clothing and realized that there was far too much blood on them to have come from the bullet hole. Haines prepped a syringe of penicillin. "Upside is you won't have gonorrhea in the morning." Swede didn't respond to the joke. His head had sunken to his chest.

Haines put an ear to Swede's mouth. His breathing was steady. He taped gauze pads over the entry and exit wounds then went into the next room for a blanket. He draped it over Swede. Swede would live to fight another day.

XXV

"So this is Chambliss." Hannisford made a show of turning his head and craning his neck. "I guess it isn't the sticks, but it's less than a mile down the road."

Poston wished Hannisford would just shut up. This was the best lead Poston had in a while, and he didn't care if the town consisted of a combination gas station general store and post office.

"Too bad it's after five o'clock," Hannisford went on. "The Chamber of Commerce is probably closed and we can't get information on our choices for fine dining and hotel accommodations."

The Hideaway Inn, the last motel they'd passed since they left the Interstate an hour before was a cinder block fleabag with half a neon sign and one car, probably the owner's parked in the lot. I don't care if I have to sleep in the Jeep, Poston thought. I'm not sharing a room with this hog.

They drove through a town square with the obligatory Confederate soldier statue and past three blocks of storefronts before the street was lined with modest houses. "Hardly looks like a place you'd find a werewolf, huh, Elroy?"

Poston grunted. "You must not have been paying attention the last twenty miles since we got off ninety-five. There's some wild country out there; pinewoods, swamps, shrub lands full of all kinds of predatory livestock. You could walk a hundred yards off the road and be lucky to find your way back again."

"When you say 'you,' you mean me, not mankind in general, right?" Poston didn't bother to answer. "Well, I never was a Boy Scout, Elroy, that's why I brought you along." He yawned. "You know the woods, and I know the dens of iniquity. Every town has one sleazy motel close by for the locals to use as a hot pillow joint. I'll find it."

Hot pillow joint? Poston thought, I'm definitely not sharing a room.

Two more miles and Hannisford's prophecy came true. The orange glow of neon announced vacancy at the Cozy Nook Motel. The place had a regrettable resemblance to the Hideaway, and as many cars in the lot.

"Doesn't look too popular," said Poston.

"That's because it's Wednesday. Wait 'til the weekend."

The room was small, the carpet threadbare, the furniture scarred with cigarette burns and the mattress lumpy, but Wednesday night in the Cozy Nook offered one advantage: there wasn't enough demand to run out the hot water. Poston stood in a steaming shower for half an hour to rinse off the road grit, the greasy smell of McDonalds food and his annoyance with Bill Hannisford.

Outside, a tan Chevy sat at the edge of the Cozy Nook's parking lot. In it, agent Dave Katz watched the motel with binoculars while his partner Ken Barnes tried to tune in a station they could both live with on the radio. Merle Haggard bleated the virtues of being an Okie from Muskogee. "I can't find anything but hillbilly music and hillbilly preachers. Tell me again why we're here."

"Because J. Edgar Hoover says so, and he signs the checks."

"But of all the places on Earth, what the hell are those two doing in

Chambliss, Georgia?"

XXVI

Slate's first impulse when the Professor—Robert Mansoor was his name—blew his cover was to walk out of the diner and put a couple of hundred miles between them, but he figured that if he could learn enough from Mansoor the risk was worth it. He could always kill him, and the woman too, if necessary, but he was walking with a toe over the edge. He knew firsthand what somebody with magical know-how could do, and he'd have to be more than careful.

Maura didn't set him up. He was sure of that. Sure, she played him because she wanted to get her hands on the *farkas ostor*, but Slate believed she didn't want him dead. Her surprise was genuine, and her continued anxiety likewise. She'd fallen into a deeper pit than she ever would have dreamed, and there was no ready way out of it.

Mansoor wanted something too, and it wasn't to see Slate dead, at least not yet, or he wouldn't have come alone to the meet. No one jumped out with a gun when he and Maura climbed into the van to follow Mansoor.

"Have you ever been to his house?" Slate asked Maura.

She shook her head. "He's very secretive. I've always met him in Mae's or some other public place."

"And you never wondered why?"

"I just thought he was eccentric. Believe me, his behavior is mild compared to some of the academics I've known." Maura was silent for a while, then said, "I can understand why you didn't tell me everything, but Robert . . ." her voice trailed off. "You really are a werewolf?"

"Four days a month, just like the National Guard."

"I have so many questions, but I'm not going to ask them. You can tell me what you want to when you want to."

"What's the point? If I tell you, what would you do? Write a book? Read a paper at some conference somewhere? You can't do anything with the information. People are looking for me; not just Pegg's followers, lots people who can't afford to let me live. If it were just me, it wouldn't matter so much, but there are others involved, and there are debts to be paid.

Everybody's got an agenda."

"I don't care if I never publish a word about this. You don't understand. I've spent half my life looking for a reason to believe that there is more to this world than the sunrise and the sunset, four seasons and a paycheck. I have to know for me, and for nobody else."

"Even so, I can't put you into the kind of danger I'm in. If the wrong people find me, they won't care if some of the bullets hit you in the process."

"Look, John—that is your name, right?"

"One of many."

"John, I'm in this now, and I'm staying. I've survived headhunters and revolutionaries. I suppose I can survive a werewolf."

"I'm not the big danger."

"Then who is?"

"Ask the Professor."

They followed Mansoor's battered green Pontiac out of the city and through its suburbs. Soon Mansoor turned off the highway and from one country road onto another, each turn leading them onto a worse road than the one before it. The van bounced and jolted on the rutted lane and Slate had to be careful to avoid breaking an axle.

The lane led to a twilit clearing in the pines and in its center stood a cottage. Chalet style, it was a story and a half of peeling paint and missing shingles. A single bare bulb lit a sagging porch. A piece of cardboard was taped over a missing windowpane. Electrical wires showed on the outside but no telephone line.

Mansoor got out of his car and started for the porch. Slate slid out of the van, put a hand under his jacket on the butt of his pistol, and said, "If you don't mind, Professor, let's all go in together."

He turned and gave Slate a mirthless grin. "Maybe you'd like to go in first unless of course, you want me to remove the wards from the doorway before you do."

Slate looked to Maura. "Protective spells," she said. "I'd let him go."

Slate nodded in agreement and Mansoor turned the knob. The door was unlocked. It swung into the darkened house and Mansoor stepped inside. A moment later a dappled mastiff the size of a small pony ambled out and sat beside the door. The dog didn't bark; in fact, it didn't move once it took up its stance. It simply stared at Slate and Maura, impassive.

Mansoor called through the doorway. "That is Janus. I'm sure you recognize the name. Come in. She won't bite you unless you give her a good reason."

Slate kept his hand on his automatic as he and Maura stepped onto the porch. The dog moved only her head as they passed. Once they were inside, Slate turned and saw that Janus had relocated herself to the center of the doorway, her onyx eyes coldly watching the newcomers.

A light came on overhead, and Slate and Maura found themselves in a living room that looked more like a rubbish heap. Books and boxes were piled atop one another and file folders lay in a corner where a heap of them had toppled, fanning papers on the floor. Dust lay everywhere. "Pardon the mess," Mansoor said, revealing the first trace of any sense of humor. "It's tough to get a maid out here."

They followed him into the kitchen where a scarred table held more files and books, these in some semblance of order. Mansoor sat in one of the chairs and waved a hand for Maura and Slate to join him.

"We are in an odd situation, Mister Slate. You need my help to control your condition. I harbor animosity toward you, yet I need your help as well. That's why I've brought you here. Some things you simply do not discuss in a diner. Here, we are protected in certain ways."

"And how do I know I can trust you?"

"You don't, any more than I can trust you. I know a little of your history. You could leap over the table and kill me with your bare hands, or simply pull out the pistol you have in your waistband and shoot me. I have knowledge that you need, and to kill me would slow your search, so you won't kill me today."

"And you just said you need my help, so you won't kill me today either. What help do you need from me?"

"I need you to help me deal with a man named Greystone." The name sent a chill of dread up Slate's spine. The wizard had infected Tommy Cimino with lycanthropy and set into motion the chain of events that brought Slate to this table. He knew little about Greystone, but what he knew was enough to make him question the equity of this alliance. He looked to Maura. Her face showed only curiosity. This is news to her too, he thought.

"My friend Derek Pegg was his adversary; they served as a check on each other. Now that Pegg is dead, Greystone is freer to pursue his own ends, which are a threat to us all."

Maura looked to Slate, who held Mansoor's stare and said to her, "Too long a story." Then to Mansoor he said, "Again, what kind of help could I give you?"

"Greystone is very interested in you, Slate. You killed his pet werewolf Laszlo Kovacks and left him without the means to make another. His need will draw him out, as will his arrogance. He cannot tolerate being beaten in any way, which is his fatal flaw. You will bring him into the open where he may be dealt with properly."

"Bait," Slate said.

Mansoor gave a curt nod. "Bait."

"So, I hang over the edge and take the chance of being killed or worse in exchange for help I may or may not live to see."

"Yes. You put it quite well."

"Greystone controlled his werewolf, so he has a *farkas ostor* too, doesn't he?"

"Yes, we have to assume that."

"What stops him from using it on me and turning me against you?"

"It only works when you are in werewolf form. You will have to deal with Greystone when the moon is out of phase in ways at which you are well-schooled."

"There are other considerations." Slate took his pack of Camels from his shirt pocket and tapped out a cigarette. "Other people have, as you put it, an interest in me, dangerous people."

"As dangerous as Greystone?"

"In their own way, yes. If I set myself out as bait, it may draw them as well."

Mansoor nodded. "That is a consideration."

"And in return for delivering Greystone, what do I get?"

"I will learn as did Pegg to use the amulet to ease your transition and to prevent you from harming yourself or others."

"And to do that, you need the book." He turned to Maura. "What did you call it? A grimoire?"

She nodded. "Yes. It's a book of spells and incantations compiled in the late nineteenth century by a man named Claude Deveraux."

"There lies another problem," Mansoor said. "The Devereaux Manuscript rests in a vault in the Duke University archives. I saw it only once during my years on the faculty. Devereaux wrote the grimoire in a personal code to prevent others from learning its secrets. The book's content is regarded to be so dangerous that no one is allowed to bring a camera, or so much as a pencil and paper into the room when viewing it for fear the spells in it be loosed on the outside world."

"If the grimoire is such a threat, why don't they destroy it?"

"Because there is always the danger that the power it represents will be needed some day to counteract a darker one."

"And you need me to steal the book and bring it to you."

"Yes. With the grimoire in my hands, I can help you and I can restore the balance of power upset by Pegg's death."

And give yourself all the powers of the book, thought Slate. It was at that moment that Slate decided first, that he would have to cooperate with Mansoor and second, that once Slate had what he needed, he would have to kill him.

XXVII

James Zampaglione heard the muffled sound of hard-soled shoes on the concrete. Somebody was outside. "Outside" to Zampaglione, "Jimmy Pags" to the members of the late Michael Monzo's crime family, was any place but the unplugged freezer where he'd been locked naked for a long time, a couple of days at least.

It had been Tuesday night when he left Sally's, the bar over on Preston Avenue, and the last thing he remembered clearly was fishing his car keys out of his pocket. He woke up in the dark in a box, knees to his chest and after a few panicked minutes of thrashing and screaming, he figured it out. He could feel the metal sides, and with nothing to do in the dark he became intimately acquainted every inch of his cramped accommodation.

The air was close, but he wouldn't suffocate. The drain spout in a bottom corner of the freezer was open. The lid gave a little when he pushed against it, so the freezer wasn't latched. Instead, it was held shut with a hasp and a padlock that rattled when he pushed against the inside of the lid.

Jimmy Pags was a big guy. It took him more than an hour and he rubbed his skin raw against the metal working himself from a fetal position into a sort of crouch. Outside the son of a bitch was whistling. When the padlock finally came off, whoever opened the freezer was going to get a big surprise.

Mister Smith opened the padlock on the lid of the unplugged freezer. Time to air out James Zampaglione. "Can't have you suffocating on us, lad," Smith said with the lilt of an Irish accent.

As soon as the shackle cleared the hasp, the lid flew open, crashing against the wall behind it, and Jimmy Pags popped up like a naked, unshaven jack-in-the-box. Pags hit Mister Smith full on the chin with a right that would have knocked out anybody else, but the tall hunchback simply grabbed Jimmy by the throat with his left hand and squeezed. Jimmy Pags' eyes bulged and his tongue popped out of his mouth.

Mister Smith swung his open right hand and slapped Jimmy so hard on the left side of his head that Jimmy's skull rang with the impact. The blow might have broken his neck if Mister Smith weren't holding it so firmly. Mister Smith backhanded Jimmy just as hard on the right side of his head and all the fight went out of him. Jimmy slumped into the freezer and lay glassy-eyed, staring upward. Mister Smith said only, "Behave."

The face Jimmy Pags saw staring down at him looked like a comic strip character. A seamed face that could be forty or fifty or sixty framed a snaggle-toothed grin and pair of bright blue eyes under caterpillar eyebrows. An unkempt mop of brown hair barely hid a pair of large, protruding ears.

"Mister Zampaglione?"

Jimmy groaned. "Water. I need water."

"Of course, you do," said Mister Smith, "and water you shall have." He aimed the nozzle of a garden hose and pulled the trigger, spraying the mobster with cold water. "Can't have you smelling up the place, now can we?"

"You bastard," Jimmy sputtered. "I'm gonna kill you."

"Not today, Mister Zampaglione, not today."

"Who the hell are you? What do you want, you freak?"

"Some conversation, Jimmy Pags. I want you to tell me about John Slate."

Jimmy snarled. "I'm telling you nothing. I'm gonna cut off your balls and stuff them down your gullet."

Mister Smith closed the lid of the freezer and slipped the shackle of the padlock through the hasp. No need to lock it because he'd be opening it again in a moment. He reached behind the freezer and picked up the plug in one hand and an extension cord in the other. He pushed the plug into the extension.

He counted to ten as a low hum accompanied by screams and the sound of a heavy body thumping against the steel walls came from the freezer then he pulled the plug. Mister Smith opened the lid and wisps of smoke rose, along with the odor of charred hair and flesh.

Zampaglione's eyes were wild. Blood trickled from the side of his mouth. He'd bitten through his tongue.

"I did a bit of rewiring, you see," said Mister Smith with a chuckle. "Not enough juice to kill you, just enough to make you wish it were." He reconnected the plug and sparks crackled. Jimmy Pags convulsed and threw his head from side to side, bouncing it off the walls of the freezer. Mister Smith unplugged the power cord and Jimmy went limp (removed comma) his chest heaving. A small fleck of foam turned pink in the blood on his lower lip.

"The water increases the conductivity, you see. Very efficient. Now, Jimmy Pags, tell me about John Slate."

Jimmy Pags said nothing. Mister Smith reached one of his long arms into the freezer and pulled back an eyelid. The eye was rolled back. Jimmy Pags was out cold and wouldn't be talking for a while. When he wakes, he'll be more talkative, thought Mister Smith, and I probably won't even have to use the electricity. He padlocked the freezer and strolled away whistling "The Irish Washerwoman," his wingtips clicking on the concrete floor.

Magic would have moved things along more quickly, but in its absence, more mundane means sufficed. Mister Smith climbed the stairs of the house to the second floor. Michael Monzo's thugs bombed and burned Greystone's townhouse in Newark and in so doing destroyed priceless books, manuscripts, and artifacts necessary to the wizard's pursuits. Restoration of his employer's power was a painful and slow process, but a necessary one and Himself was a determined fellow.

At the end of the upstairs hallway, Mister Smith brushed aside the curtains and looked out on the rolling fields of the Pennsylvania countryside. The farmhouse was a poor second to the Newark townhouse for comfort but more secure since he could take protective measures in the fields and forest that surrounded the property, measures he could never have taken in a city neighborhood. Let them come, he thought; if they dare. The things that prowled the forest were as swift and silent as they were deadly.

Before he could knock at the door a voice that was much an echo in his head as a sound to his ear said, "Come."

Mister Smith entered a room curtained to the point of near darkness against the bright sunlight. Behind a desk at one end of the room sat Greystone, dubbed the Whisperer by one of his late underlings because his voice was nearly inaudible but heard nonetheless.

"What have you learned?"

"Nothing yet, but he'll tell me what he knows very soon. When he wakes up I should think."

The Whisperer steepled his fingers. "Have you located any others of

Monzo's crew?"

"Two more. They fled Newark but I've tracked them to Philadelphia."

The Whisperer nodded. "It frustrates me to use such common means, but until my power is restored, they will suffice."

Mister Smith bowed respectfully and left the room closing the door behind him.

Two hours later, Mister Smith revisited the cellar and found Jimmy Pags most cooperative. Three hours later, Mister Smith, in his brown suit and wingtips was busy carting the mobster over his shoulder away from the house and into the forest. Jimmy wasn't dead, but it didn't matter.

Zampaglione had given Mister Smith the name of a target. "I only heard the name once, the redneck game warden who shot Paco and the others in the Barrens. One of the guys said Monzo wanted him dead. Poston. Some hick first name . . .Elroy. Elroy Poston. That's it."

Mister Smith hunched forward and dropped Jimmy Pags to the ground with a thud. He listened for a few seconds and heard no birds, no animals, only the rustle of the wind in the trees. The Guardians were nearby. No doubt they smelled the flesh and blood and were already circling the clearing. Mister Smith puckered his lips and whistled a song like no other. In a moment, shadows in the shape of men made of smoke drifted into the clearing. They swarmed over Jimmy Pags and for a moment became one gray mass.

There were screams followed by whimpers followed by silence. When the Guardians drifted away, Jimmy Pags was gone forever.

XXVIII

After a night and half a day, Haines figured that Swede's wound was clean. He was lucky. The slug didn't fragment or chip any bones. His temperature was normal, and although he was still weak from blood loss, he was in good shape. He still wasn't strong enough to make a trek back into the swamp where he'd been shot, and Haines and Singer would have to look long and hard to find the location.

The story Swede told about springing the traps and killing the two locals in self-defense rang true with Haines and Singer, and they agreed they'd probably have done the same thing, but what worried Haines was the possibility that if the bodies were found the locals might suspect them. So far they didn't pay much attention to four guys living in a hunting camp in the swamp, but this business might change everything.

Singer came in from the porch. "Swede gave me a pretty good idea of where he ran into those rednecks. He wasn't exactly subtle coming back here, so I might be able to reverse his trail and find the bodies."

"If we're lucky the local livestock took care of them for us."

Singer nodded. "If we're lucky."

"Any place you find one of those traps, reset it. Don't give some sharp cop a motive in case they do find the bodies."

"Good idea." Singer went into the bedroom and came out in camo fatigues and jungle boots. "Take good care of the patient," he said, loading shells into his sawed-off Ithaca pump. A groan of the screen door and Singer was gone.

Like any of the team, Swede could not only pass unnoticed through a forest but could do it without leaving a trace behind That is, when he was hitting on all his cylinders. Shot and delirious, he'd left signs that a Boy Scout could spot, broken tree branches, size thirteen boot prints, trampled moss and occasional blood stained foliage. As he followed Swede's trail, he covered the traces as best he could. It was easier than Singer thought to find the sprung trap chained to the cypress tree.

He reset the trap and daubed mud over the metal. The dead possum left as bait was picked almost to the bones by whatever happened along during the night. Singer found tracks in the mud at the water's edge. He recognized the imprint of Swede's boot and saw the tracks of two others, the same rubber boots but different sizes mixed in. The drag marks in the mud jibed with Swede's story. Singer picked up a tree branch and poked at the shallow water. Nothing out of the ordinary. No bodies. The sun shone through the trees and the birds sang as if nothing had ever happened here.

Singer scanned the surface of the water and about thirty feet away and saw what looked like a submerged log but he realized was an eight-foot alligator. "*Bon appétit,*" he said with a salute. Likely the gator had the bodies stashed in a den under the banks nearby. Singer swept the ground with the tree branch to cover the tracks, including his own, checked the area around the trap one last time for any traces of Swede, and left the way he came.

He'd been on the trail for about fifteen minutes when he heard voices, maybe two hundred yards away. He climbed a tall cypress tree and nestled into a crouch behind a veil of Spanish moss. It took a while, but a group of men appeared, spread about twenty feet apart and carrying rifles. Singer thought they might be hunters until he saw the campaign hat on the furthest man's head and the shield on his chest: Georgia Patrol.

Singer waited a full ten minutes before he came down from the tree to make sure the search party was long gone and no stragglers were following them. This, he thought might be a problem. He took twice as long getting back to camp as he had on the trip out, making sure he was unseen and unheard.

XXIX

Duke University's Library Building looked more like a Gothic Cathedral than a library, and like so many buildings built to resemble medieval architecture, its structure presented medieval security problems. If he did the job right, no one would know he'd been there or stolen the book for a long time, long after Slate was back in Chambliss with the grimoire.

The rare books vault in Duke University's Main Library Building was a misnomer. Its imposing door had a tumbler lock like a safe, but its walls were ordinary construction. The library's emergency exits had simple panic bar doors equipped with burglar alarms, more to alert the library personnel if a patron tried to escape with a book without checking it out than to thwart intruders.

The door alarms weren't much as security went, but they were loud, as Slate learned when a student opened one of the emergency exits. The klaxon blared only as long as the door was open, but it was noisy enough to be heard for blocks. The exit doors would be okay as an escape route in a pinch, but unless he could cut the power to one of the alarms in advance, the emergency doors were no good for entry.

• • •

Not wanting to be seen in the building, he sent Maura with a camera to photograph the door to the vault and the emergency exits and while she took the film to a Foto-Hut for express developing, he sat in the van a block away with his scope, watching the comings and goings of the library's patrons. The building had no uniformed personnel during the daytime; only the librarians guarded the portals.

Maura returned with the prints a few hours later, and although they were dim and in some cases blurry, they told him what he needed to know. "The emergency exit doors all have surface wiring from a trigger at the top of the door to the klaxon mounted beside it," he said. "Another surface mounted cable connects the horn to one of two sockets in a house current wall outlet. It looks as if there's no connection to any central unit; each door alarm is independent of the others."

"Can they be disabled?" Maura asked.

"Easier than you think. Is there a hardware store close by? We need some plastic tape. And find me a wire coat hanger."

A half hour later, Maura was back in the library standing before the ground level exit in the southwest corner of the building, chosen because it was partially hidden on the outside by tall arborvitae shrubs that she could see through the wire-reinforced glass. She heard people walking through the stacks behind her and the occasional murmur of voices on the floor, but she saw no one nearby, so she crouched, took a deep breath, and pulled the alarm plug from the outlet, ready to bolt at the first sign of trouble.

Nothing happened. No alarm went off. No armed guards came running. Maura let out the breath and pulled the roll of clear plastic packing tape from her bag. She cut off two small pieces with a pair of nail clippers and stuck them over the tines of the plug. "Do it long ways," Slate had told her. If you wrap them sideways, the tape may pull away when you put the plug back into the socket. One tine would do the trick, but do them both to be safe."

The tape covered the tines completely and Maura pressed the overlapping sticky sides face to face. She gently slid the plug back into the socket, straightened up and took another deep breath before she pushed the panic bar and opened the door. Silence. No one seemed to notice that the door had been opened.

Back at the van, Slate was leaning back in the driver's seat, eyes closed. She opened the door and slid in. "It worked."

Slate nodded. "Good."

"I've never been a burglar before. It was kind of scary and exciting at the same time. What do we do now?"

Slate looked at his watch. "Now we wait."

The library locked its doors each night at eleven o'clock. The janitorial staff finished its routine of sweeping floors and emptying wastebaskets by midnight and the place was dark by one o'clock.

Since campus unrest in protest of the Viet Nam action had become a larger issue, university security had diverted many of its resources to the hot locations on campus, Old Main, the R.O.T.C. building and the administration complex. The library and the academic buildings got less attention from the uniformed security patrols.

The night before Slate had watched from the bushes as the security personnel, on foot and in the university prowl cars made their rounds. The foot patrolman was alone and his job seemed to consist largely of checking exterior doors to see whether they were locked. The officer on duty wore the standard Detex time clock like a thick canteen on a strap over his shoulder and walked from station to station around the campus recording the time of his visit to each with a coded key that hung from a chain at each station.

The library's key station was a metal flap attached to the wall near the main entrance. In the dim light of lantern-like sconces on either side of the door, three times Slate watched the night patrolman open the flap, insert the key in the Detex clock, replace the key, circle the building with his flashlight bobbing and go on his way to the next key station.

The wild card was the prowl car or cars. Slate counted three different cars and drivers over the course of the night driving by at irregular times and periodically shining a spotlight into shadowy areas. Two of the cars were campus rent-a-cops; the third was a city cruiser. The possibility that a random patrol would pass and he might be seen meant the front door wasn't the best option, which is why he chose the emergency exit as his likeliest entry point.

"Can I ask you how you know how to do all this stuff?" Maura said around a bite of a cheeseburger. She had gone out for food and came back with burgers, fries, and cans of Coca-Cola.

"Loss protection means keeping people from breaking in and stealing things. Brown and Root paid me to know how the bad guys do it so I could keep them from doing it."

She nodded and took another bite from her burger, unconvinced by his answer but knowing better than to pursue the subject.

...she slid the plug back into the socket...

XXX

The police cruiser was a big Ford Crown Victoria with a whip antenna that bowed from the back bumper to just over the driver's door. The sides were emblazoned with the insignia of the Georgia Patrol. The car bumped and lurched into the camp in the late afternoon, twin four-barrel carbs on the 460 interceptor engine sucking down fuel by the gallon. It pulled up into the yard and two uniformed men climbed out.

Singer, Haines, and Swede had heard it coming from a half mile away and were sitting on the porch of the cabin drinking beer when the officers strolled up. Swede had taken off his sling and his right arm rested on the porch railing. He had to wrap his fingers around a Budweiser can with his other hand. He was still a little pale but his ruddy complexion hid it well enough.

The cops both smiled affably but behind their mirrored aviator glasses, Haines knew their eyes were taking in every detail of the camp. "Afternoon, fellas," said the shorter one, a corporal whose name tag said, "Beaudry".

All three nodded and Haines took the lead. "Hello, officers. What can we do for you?"

"I'm Corporal Alan Beaudry. This here's Tom Grover. Who're you, fellows?" Beaudry's accent turned all of his "ows" into "as" and his "ers' into ""uhs."

Haines swept a hand around the porch. "I'm Mike Crawford, this is Tom Shultz, and the big guy's Ray Haggerty."

Beaudry took off his sunglasses and stared at each of them in turn, fixing their faces and names in his mind. "We're hoping you might be able to help us out. A couple of local boys went missing yesterday. We found their truck but no trace of them. We hoped you might have seen them."

"Tell you the truth, officer," said Haines, "we don't see too many people out here. About the only time we do is when we make a run to Red's for groceries and beer."

Grover was looking back toward the dock. "You take that airboat to Red's?"

"Yep. It's the quickest way to get there."

Beaudry made a show of looking around. "You don't have a car?"

"We have a van but our partner's got it today. We have that and the bike over there." Haines pointed to a mud-splattered yellow dirt bike parked under a tree.

Beaudry nodded. "Yeah, after driving up that road I can understand why you'd use the boat. Anyway, these boys that are missing . . . "

"Who are they?" Singer said.

"Their names are Jack Martin and Connor Jones. They're a couple of swamp rats, spend most of their time hunting and trapping out here."

"Don't know the names. Got a picture?"

"Not yet, but if they don't turn up, I'll be back with one. Martin's about five-foot-eight, dark hair and a scraggly beard. Jones is a little taller, lean, long sandy hair like a hippie." He turned to Swede. "No offense," Swede grinned.

Singer said, "You said you found a truck; was it near here?"

"A mile or two north. Looks like they were checking traps. Actually, we didn't find it ourselves. Jack told his girlfriend where he and Connor were going. He didn't come back when he said he would, and she drove out there and found the truck. She waited 'til after dark and when they didn't show, she called the Sheriff. When they didn't show by morning, he called us."

"Do people go missing around here often?"

Beaudry shook his head. "Nope, but that swamp's a dangerous place. A dozen ways to get killed out there." He paused. "And that's just by Nature."

"Well, if we see them we'll let you know right away."

Beaudry nodded. "I heard Curt Parker sold the place a while back. You fellows plan on staying here a while?"

Haines smiled. "We were all in the Army together. We came back from Nam and found this place. We're thinking about running hunting and fishing tours."

Beaudry said, "Marine MP here. I just missed Viet Nam. Got out of the service a little too early."

"Count yourself lucky," Singer said. "Nothing over there but trouble."

The radio squawked and Grover leaned into the cruiser to listen to the call. Beaudry took a last look around.

"If you see those men or any trace they've been around, you call us. That's a CB antenna isn't it?" He pointed to the roof of the cabin. "And a short wave antenna too?"

"Yep. No phone out here."

"We monitor channel nine on the Citizens Band."

He started toward the cruiser and stopped. He turned and said to Swede,

"Better drink that beer soon, buddy, or it'll be warm as piss when you get to it." Without another word the patrolmen climbed into the cruiser and in a moment the car was bouncing and jolting down the rutted lane.

"Beaudry looks like a handful," said Haines.

"Not exactly that fat-bellied sheriff you see in the Dodge commercials," said Singer. "His partner's no Barney Fife either. While Beaudry was keeping our attention, Grover was jotting down the registry number on the airboat."

"He'll be back," said Swede.

"Yep," said Haines. "He's sharp. We need to comb over the place and make sure there's nothing illegal in case Beaudry brings a warrant with him next time."

XXXI

Watching Hannisford eat was like watching a cement mixer churning a load of mortar. "For God's sake," said Poston. "Close your mouth when you chew." He wanted to just pack his gear and buy a bus ticket back Jersey, but he couldn't afford to let the lead go without checking it out. They were sitting in a booth in Jack's Pizza, the only pizza shop in Chambliss.

The pizza was almost gone and Poston had eaten only two of the twelve slices. Hannisford had gobbled down eight and was reaching for a ninth. "This pizza isn't bad," Hannisford said. "I expected it to come with possum belly instead of pepperoni."

"You watch too much *Beverly Hillbillies*," Poston said. "Civilization arrived in Georgia about the same year it hit Boston. Maybe you didn't notice but the TV in the motel gets all three networks."

Hannisford laughed and folded a slice of the pizza in two and stuffed it into his mouth to take a bite. He pointed to the last slice in the flat cardboard box. "You want the last one?" he said around the wad of dough.

"Nah, you enjoy it," Poston said. And maybe if I'm lucky, he thought, you'll swallow the last glob of cholesterol it takes to shut your arteries down once and for all and put me out of my misery.

"We'll meet those two high school kids at seven and get their story. We can go for a look around at the site tomorrow. I can try setting up a couple of trip wire cams like I used before. Maybe I'll get lucky again."

Outside in a corner of the parking lot, a tan Chevy Impala sat with two men in the front seat. "I'm getting hungry, Katz," said Barnes, the agent watching the pair through the front window of the pizza shop with binoculars. That pizza smells good all the way over here. Maybe we could get one when those two leave."

"Okay by me. We just can't let the subjects see us and we can't lose them."

"When they take off, you follow them and see where they go and I'll order the pizza. You loop back around when they drop anchor and pick me up."

"You and half the pizza."

"Sure, half the pizza."

"Sounds like a good plan in theory, but what if they head back to Jersey?"

"I'll just have to eat the whole thing myself."

"Get down. They're coming out now."

XXXII

The Frosty Freeze was a neon island in the night at eight p.m., and when Jake rolled up on his bike Billy was waiting at one of the picnic tables under the glowing yellow eaves of the drive-in restaurant. Jake shut off his engine and dropped the kickstand of the Yamaha. He ambled over to the table and plopped down on the bench. "Not here yet, huh?"

"Not yet. What do we do if they don't show?"

"I have the number for *Unidentified's* office in New York. We can call and see what's what. I'm betting they'll be here any minute, though. That Hannisford guy I talked to today sounded really hot for the interview."

"Did he say what kind of car they were driving?

"Yeah, a gray Jeep Wagoneer."

"You getting anything to eat?"

"Not yet. I'll wait 'til they get here. They're on an expense account. Let them buy it. It's all part of the game."

It was another fifteen minutes before the beat-up grey Jeep pulled into the Frosty Freeze. By then Jake had given in and bought a chocolate milkshake for himself. When the fat guy with the glasses and the lean guy in the denim jacket and the army cap climbed out of the Jeep, Jake said out of the corner of his mouth, "Let me do the talking."

The fat guy grinned and said, "Hi, is one of you Jake Smalley?"

Billy nudged him and said under his breath, "Why's he asking for you, not me? I'm the one who saw the werewolves."

Jake said out of the corner of his mouth, "Because I sent in the stuff. Now let me handle this," then in a louder voice, "Yeah, that's me."

"I'm Bill Hannisford from *Unidentified*. This fellow is Elroy Poston."

"This is Billy Davis. You guys hungry? The burgers are good here."

"We already ate," Hannisford said. "Maybe another time."

Jake's face fell. So much for the free food.

Hannisford sat on the bench of the picnic table and the two-by-sixes bowed under his weight. The other guy, Poston, didn't sit. Jake disliked Poston from the second he saw him, and he could tell Poston didn't much care for him or Billy, either. For that matter, he didn't seem to like Hannisford any better.

"So tell us your story from the start."

"I took the photos of the tracks. Billy's the one who actually saw the werewolves."

Hannisford took a cassette recorder from his knapsack and set it on the table. "You don't mind if I record this do you? I mean, it's an interview."

"Well, I guess . . ."

"Wait a minute. We haven't talked about money yet," said Jake.

"We'll give you a standard contract if we decide to use the story. The photo's already accepted and I have a check for you right here." Hannisford pulled a wallet out of his hip pocket and rifled through the back compartment 'til he found a folded check. He uncreased it and held it up in front of him. "There you go, pal, one hundred dollars." Jake reached for the check and Hannisford held it back. "It's yours if the story checks out. After all, the tracks could have been fakes, not that you'd do something like that, but maybe somebody else did just for a joke. After all, it was Halloween week wasn't it?"

"Hey, man," Billy said indignantly. "I saw those things. And I can tell you, they sure looked real enough to me. We were out on the Knob, my girlfriend Roxy and me . . ." Billy was on a roll and shook off Jake's restraining hand. Neither noticed that Hannisford had pressed the record button on the cassette machine.

"Roxy Barton?" Hannisford cut in.

"Uh, yeah. How did you know?"

"We got a letter from her the day after we heard from you guys. She wants to sell us her story too."

Billy and Jake looked at each other. "Oh shit," said Jake. Billy's mouth hung open.

"That doesn't mean we won't use your account; after all, you have the picture as proof and she doesn't. She just has a story. That's why we want to check it all out to make sure. And anyway, you guys wrote in first, so we came to you first."

Poston rolled his eyes. Hannisford should be selling used cars. He was a fat bum, but he sure knew how to play these kids. Dangle the money under their noses, let them know they're competing with the girl then make them think we're on their side, not hers. He said, "Can you take us to the place where you took the picture in daylight; let us have a look around?"

"Yeah, we can do that," Jake said, regaining some of his composure. "We'll show you. We put a rock over the track to cover it, and it's still there." He was glad he'd thought of that detail.

"Good deal," said Hannisford. "Now, Billy, tell us what happened."

Billy fell right into the net, his eyes getting wider and his voice louder, his gestures more expansive as he told the story of his encounter, and Hannisford's tape recorder got every word. He pulled out a camera and took a half-dozen shots of the boys and that concluded the meeting.

As the Jeep pulled out of the Frosty Freeze, Poston said, "That was devious. You told them you came to them first but you didn't tell them the girl already sent you her story."

"Hey, did I lie?" Hannisford grinned. "I've been in this game for a long time, Elroy. Trust me. I know how to play it."

You know how to play it, thought Poston, but trust you? No way in hell.

"The girl's story lines up with his except for one little detail."

"What's that?"

"Billy the Kid pissed his pants. I can understand why he wouldn't say so. If it were me, I wouldn't admit that even if it did happen."

If you saw what I saw in the Barrens, thought Poston, you'd've gone a step further. "But the stories are pretty much identical."

"Yeah," Hannisford said with a nod. "Unless the three of them are in cahoots. But based on the looks on the boys' faces when we told them about Roxy, I'd say they had no idea she was in the mix. They both looked like I hit them across the forehead with a two-by-four."

"I think you're probably right," Poston said. And I hope you are, he thought, because if that track is real, I won't need you anymore, you fat bastard, and that would be a gift. "When do we talk to the girl, this Roxy?"

Hannisford looked at his watch. "Tomorrow morning at ten, unless I get lost, but in a town the size of Chambliss, that's unlikely."

• • •

"It's a good thing this town's as small as it is," said Katz, still behind the wheel of the tan Impala. And it's a good thing Hannisford and Poston didn't head for the Interstate."

"Yeah, but the pizza was worth the risk." Barnes wiped his mouth with a napkin and looked across the road at the two teenage boys sitting at the Frosty Freeze. "We waiting for them to leave?"

"Nah, they aren't important just now, but we'll check them out later. I have the plate number on the motorcycle. We can run it and find out where the short one lives. Besides, I'm guessing if we go the public library tomorrow, we'll find both their faces in a high school yearbook and take it from there."

"What do you think the connection is, dope maybe?"

"Maybe," said Katz. "But who knows?" He started the engine. "They're little fish. Let's follow the middle ones. If we're lucky maybe they'll lead us to the big ones."

XXXIII

By midnight Maura was stiff and her back and legs hurt from sitting in the van. Slate sat like a mannequin, his eyes either on the building when it was his turn or closed when it was her turn to watch. The last of the cleaning crew left and a uniformed guard locked the doors. Dim lights shone in the foyer and outside the front door, and spots lit the facade of the building, leaving the sides and rear in shadow.

"Remember, if the security people show up, and it could happen, start the van and drive it with the lights off for three blocks east and wait for me. If I don't show in fifteen minutes, go to that diner where we met Mansoor. It's open all night, right?"

Maura nodded.

"Sit in a booth near the pay phone. I got the number when we were there to meet Mansoor. If I'm arrested, I get one phone call. That'll be it, and I'll tell you what to do."

"How do think of all this stuff?"

"Good training and lots of practice." Slate took a dark ski mask from his pocket and pulled it onto his head. He rolled it from the bottom so that it looked like an ordinary watch cap. "After I get out, climb over to the driver's seat." He opened the door and stepped out.

"Hey, John," Maura called. "Good luck."

"Thanks, but if I do this right, luck'll have nothing to do with it."

Once he was around the side of the building, Slate pulled the mask down to cover his face. His dark clothes blended into the shrubbery and shadows that all but hid the emergency exit from the street.

When he reached the exit, Slate straightened the coat hanger leaving the hook at one end. The door was tight against the steel jamb on the top and sides but had a rubber strip across the sill as a weather seal. He pushed the hooked end of the hanger between the weather strip and the bottom of the door until it was halfway through, then he pulled upward, bending a right angle in the wire.

He could see the panic bar through the pane of chicken-wired glass. Manipulating the coat hanger from the outside, Slate dropped the hook over the bar. Once it was secure, he pulled backward on the hanger, drawing the wire to the outside. The panic bar swung downward and Slate heard a click. The door swung open and he was in.

The library was ghostly, silent, lit by only the yellow eyes of the mandatory fire code emergency lights. Slate stole quietly through the stacks, alert for any sound other than his own breathing and the soft pad of his rubber-soled shoes on the tiles.

Slate had memorized the map Maura drew for him that led to an innocuous corner of the third floor of the building. Light from a street lamp outside the nearby window dimly lit the hallway. The door he found there was a standard size. It was steel with an oak veneer stained to match the other woodwork on the floor. Instead of a knob, a turn handle rested under a combination dial.

The mechanism was a recent vintage, but Slate believed he could crack it easily enough. He put a shot glass against the door and pressed his ear against it, spinning the numbered dial to clear the tumblers. The shot glass trick was an old one, but it worked better than a stethoscope; he could hear every tick of the mechanism inside the door.

Five tries later he began to doubt his skills. One more shot. He put his ear to the door and concentrated on the grind and click. He stopped suddenly, his senses alert. He heard nothing but he smelled the faint odor of cigarette smoke.

"You won't get in that way, my friend."

Slate spun from the door, his pistol already in his hand.

The deep voice said, "Easy, friend. I'm not the enemy."

Slate strained his eyes and could make out only the silhouette of a tall thin man. He cocked the hammer of the automatic. "You know that sound?" Silence. "Step closer to the window."

The newcomer did and what Slate saw was an old man in a rumpled suit, his unkempt hair swirling around his head like cotton candy. Heavy horn-rimmed glasses perched on a long nose that pointed like an arrow to the three-day growth of beard whitening his chin. He clutched a book in both hands and held it between him and Slate's pistol like a shield. "Don't shoot a poor old man. Amos Mackenzie at your service. I won't be so impolite as to ask who you are.

"Even if you did open that door, the alarm inside would bring the gendarmes running before you could disable it," he said. "If you will allow me," he set the book on the floor and Slate stepped back. The old man's bony fingers twirled the combination dial. "This lock has an override sequence in the event that the original is lost or forgotten. That should do it."

He reached for the handle and Slate clamped an arm on his wrist. "Hold it. What about the alarm?"

Although Slate couldn't see it, he could sense the old man's smile in the dark. "Twenty seconds, my good man. The alarm doesn't sound for twenty seconds to allow the staff to turn it off." Slate let go of his arm and the old man pushed down the handle. "Right this way." Inside the door, the old man threw a switch and overhead lights came on. Under the switch was a small metal box surface-mounted to the wall. Slate could hear the whirr of clockwork inside it. The old man threw a switch on the side of the box and the noise stopped. He stepped away from the door. "Welcome to the vault."

The room held ranks of locked steel cabinets, but these weren't the standard institutional fare. Slate could tell at a glance that they were fireproof and would be tough to break into with a sledge hammer and a cold chisel.

He moved from one to the next scanning the door plates for number 19.

When he found it, he reached in his pocket for his lock picks. "Don't go to all the trouble," the old man said. Slate turned to see him holding a ring of small brass keys. "They keep the spares in a fake outlet beside the desk."

The old man might be crazy, but he was right. "How do you know all of this?"

"Because until a few years ago I was a tenured professor of History in this revered institution." Mackenzie's voice dripped with sarcasm. "But when I started exposing all the Commies and the leftists in the faculty and the administration, I became *persona non grata*. So, I was unceremoniously discharged. But up to that point, I was chairman of the Library Committee, and its secrets are no secret to me.

"After they fired me, I haunted the stacks writing screeds in the books to debunk all the fraudulent propaganda the Left spews out. Then the Library barred me, so now I have to sneak in here at night to do my work."

He held out the ring to Slate, one key pinched between his thumb and finger. "This will open Number 19."

"I have to ask, why are you helping me?"

"The enemy of my enemy is my friend, and my friend, Duke University is my enemy."

Slate turned the key in the lock and the cabinet door swung open. The manuscripts and books were shelved in individual heavy cardboard containers. Slate found the one labeled "Devereaux Manuscript" and took it from the shelf. The book was as Mansoor described it; a leather-bound journal the size of a small town telephone book with a locking hasp holding its covers closed.

Slate put the empty storage container back on the shelf and closed the cabinet door. "Smart lad," said Mackenzie."If you put everything else back the way you found it, no one will know anything's gone for a long time if ever."

Mackenzie put away the keys. "Out you go, my friend. I have to reset the alarm and lock the door." As Slate stepped into the hallway, he heard a door slam below and two pairs of feet on the tiles. Muffled voices drifted up the stairwell. "They said they saw fire on the second floor."

"Oh dear," said Mackenzie. "I shouldn't have lit my cigarette so close to the windows." He turned to Slate. "Hide up here until they're gone. I'll go give myself up. I'm just a crazy old man, so they think. They won't even hold me; they'll just take me home, but you, my friend, I'm not so sure." He picked up the book he'd set by the door and hurried at a fast trot to the staircase.

"Thank you," Slate whispered, although he didn't think Mackenzie heard him.

Ten minutes later, Slate saw two campus cops gently escorting Mackenzie by his elbows to the prowl car. As they guided him into the back seat, he raised his hand above the roof of the car and his long fingers formed a vee.

Slate slipped out the emergency exit. Maura would have left as soon as the prowl car pulled up, and by now she would have gone to the rendezvous point, the diner. Slate pulled off the ski mask and wadded it into his pocket, tucked the grimoire into the waistband of his trousers under his sweater, and started walking.

Mae's looked more crowded than Slate would have expected, but this was a college town on a Friday and it probably had more than its share of night-owls. Through the windows, he saw Maura sitting in a booth at the back near the phone. Mansoor was sitting across from her.

Slate found a phone booth three blocks up the street and called the diner. The phone rang four times and Maura picked it up. "Hello?"

"Why is Mansoor there? I told you we do this alone."

"He was here when I came in. What was I supposed to do?"

Slate was silent for a moment, thinking, long enough for Maura to say, "John? Are you there?"

"No names," he snapped. "Get in the van and drive east. Now. You'll see me."

"Did you get it?"

"Leave Mansoor there. Don't even go back to the booth."

"What if he tries to follow me?"

"He won't. I slashed all four of his tires."

In five minutes, Slate saw the white van coming. When it was almost to the corner where he was hiding in the shadows, he stepped out into view and waved an arm. Maura, taken by surprise, slammed on the brakes and the van screeched to a stop. He yanked the door open and jumped inside. "Turn North for the Interstate."

"Where are we going?"

Slate didn't answer.

Anxiety crept over Maura's face. "Are you going to tell me what's going on?"

Slate looked over to her and took a Lucky Strike from his pack. He tapped it on the dash, put it in his mouth and lit it. "You've heard the joke with the punch line, 'It's top secret and if I tell you then I'll have to kill you.'"

She nodded. "Yeah?"

Slate took a deep drag on the cigarette. He stared out the windshield into the night. "It's no joke. We need to get about a hundred miles away from here."

XXXIV

Maura woke in the front seat of the van. Through the windshield, she saw a parking lot full of cars and the front of a Winn-Dixie supermarket. Big white paper signs in the window touted the Saturday special: T-Bone and Sirloin steak for ninety-nine cents a pound. She rubbed her aching eyes and like some magic trick, Slate appeared in front of the van with a brown paper grocery sack. Maura was too tired to be startled. He held the sack against his hip while he fished the keys from the pocket of his jeans and unlocked the driver door. Slate handed in the bag and said, "Breakfast. Now all we have to do is find coffee."

Maura drove the first two hours the night before as Slate told her an incredible tale of werewolves, wizards, gangsters, and spies that ran from Laos to Newark to the Jersey Pine Barrens. "I'm telling you this," he had said, "Because I need your help and you have to know what risks are involved. When I'm done, you'll have to decide whether you want to go on."

When she was about to fall asleep at the wheel, Slate took over and she slept. Her sleep was uneasy and several times she started awake to see Slate's impassive face in the green glow of the dashboard lights driving the van like a robot, eyes front and fully awake and aware.

"Where are we?"

"Georgia."

She opened her door and stepped out of the van. Maura groaned as she stretched and bent forward at the waist. She put her hands at the small of her back and straightened then twisted her torso left then right, cracking her spine into alignment. The sun was pale behind clouds that wouldn't rain that day, just make the world look dim.

She had chosen to go with Slate and help him. Her common sense screamed "No!" but her curiosity overrode it. "In for a penny, in for a buck," she told Slate, although she knew that from that moment forward she'd be in more danger than she'd ever been in her life.

Slate sat in the driver's seat watching her. This had been a crucial moment, her first real opportunity to bolt. If she didn't run while he was in the Winn-Dixie, she was in for the full ride.

Maura turned in a circle, taking in the cars and pickup trucks, Saturday shoppers with carts full of groceries, families with children as if taking one last look at the world she knew. She climbed back into the van and pulled the door closed behind her. "Let's find a gas station. I need a bathroom."

Slate parked the van between two tractor trailers at the Flying W to make it invisible from the highway. The truck stop coffee was brutal but helpful. Ideas pin-balled around Maura's head and one came into focus. "You knew who I was before you met me." A statement not a question. "You came to Manville looking for me."

"Guilty as charged. I read your book and your profile from articles I found in the *Biography Index*. I also read in the back files of the *Manville Chronicle* that you were on sabbatical. I wasn't quite sure how to approach you, but things worked out. Your contact with Mansoor was a bonus I didn't count on."

"But if he's a bonus, as you call him, why did we leave him in Durham?"

"Because he was a little too eager to get his hands on the book. He has his own agenda going, and I don't trust him. I'm taking a chance on you as it is." He reached behind the seat and pulled up a knapsack. "Here's the book." He handed Maura the journal and she held it with a kind of reverence. Slate had already picked the lock. She undid the hasp and opened the grimoire with a crackle of dried leather. The pages were written in dark ink in a very precise hand with occasional notes jotted in the margins. She leafed through four or five pages and said, "I can't read this. Like Mansoor said, it's written in some kind of code."

"Leave that to us."

Maura stared at page after page of secrets in her lap as Slate started the van and pulled out of the truck stop and back onto the highway. Halfway through the journal, she found the drawing of the *farkas ostor*.

XXXV

The next afternoon, Hannisford and Poston sat in the weak rays of a November sun on a bench with a view of the Confederate soldier statue that looked down on them with a stern expression. He clutched his rifle in both hands ready to fire it or swing it like a club at anyone who dared invade the square and disturb its peace.

Hannisford chuckled. "If they're going to put up a statue, they oughta put up one worth looking at, maybe some naked broad with big boobs. Now the Greeks, they knew how to dress up a public space."

Poston finally had enough. "You overgrown turd," he said. "You don't know what honor is, what sacrifice is all about, what war means to people, especially if it rips through their lives like a tornado. All you know is your fat, stupid self. Do you have any idea what Sherman's March did to this town?"

Hannisford stared at Poston for a good three seconds, his face a startled mask. Then he burst out laughing, slapping his chubby thigh. "Words of wisdom from the game warden. You're right. The statue is noble." He stood and opened his camera bag. He pulled the lens cap from one of his oversized Nikons and peered through the viewfinder at the statue. The shutter clicked and Hannisford grinned.

"There you go, Elroy, preserved for posterity. I'll print you up a half dozen." Poston glared at him and he went on. "There's something I've been wondering; do you plan to do something major with your life, I mean in a historical sense. Is there some reason the Jetsons named their boy Elroy after you?" Poston was taking a deep breath to answer when Hannisford pointed across the square and said, "Hey, look. I'll bet that's our girl coming now."

Roxy was standing, uncertain, staring across the square at them. She was in full hippie regalia today and looked like a fugitive from the Summer of Love. "This is great," said Hannisford with no trace of irony. "What a picture she'll make, especially side by side on the same page with the clean-cut jock." He waved and shouted, "Roxy?"

She waved back hesitantly and started across the square. Hannisford said aside to Poston, "Maybe you should ask her what she thinks about the statue. I bet she'd have a few choice words about war."

Poston gritted his teeth. He remembered all too well getting off the boat in Bakersfield with his unit and being met by a gang of kids dressed like her, bell-bottomed jeans and tie-dyed shirts, who spat on them and called them "baby-killers." They and Hannisford wore different costumes but they were all cut from the same irreverent bolt of cloth.

"Do you think she's over eighteen?"

"What?"

"Roxy." He pointed to the approaching girl. "If she isn't, we'll have to get her parents to sign the release for her story and her picture." He leered. "Just being professional, Elroy."

As he stood, Poston thought, if I'm going to do anything important with my life, it'll probably involve removing this asshole's DNA from the human gene pool.

"Hi, Roxy. I'm Bill Hannisford from "Unidentified". This is Elroy Poston."

Hannisford shook hands with her and held on for a second too long. Poston could barely see Roxy's eyes behind her granny glasses, but the look he saw told him she was wary of Hannisford. The kid had good instincts. He gave her hand a quick shake and let it go.

"Do you want to talk here or would you rather go someplace else?"

The question was innocuous, but coming out of Hannisford's mouth, it sounded sleazy.

"Here is okay, I guess."

Don't go anywhere with strange men, even if you might make some cash, Poston thought. Although the faint scent of pot clung to her clothes like cologne, the kid was savvier than she looked.

"Well, then, let's sit down and talk." Hannisford sat at the end of the bench and patted the space beside him. Poston stayed on his feet, his expression looking a little like the Confederate soldier's.

Hannisford pulled out his cassette machine and pushed the record button. "Interview with Roxy Barton—"

"Roxanne."

Hannisford's eyebrows raised.

"I'd rather you call me Roxanne, and that's how I want it in the magazine."

Good for you, kid, thought Poston. Make it on your own terms.

Poston nodded emphatically. "Roxanne it is. Interview with Roxanne Barton of Chambliss, Georgia, November 15th, 1969. Now, Roxanne." He emphasized the name. "Tell me about the werewolves."

Across the square, Billy watched as Roxy talked with the men from the

"Do you want to talk here…?"

magazine. He couldn't hear her words, but he knew they were unraveling his whole life. Once her version of the incident on the Knob got out, he'd be finished in this town. His senior year would be hell. He spun on his heel and started for Jake's house. Jake would know how to head this off.

On the other side of the square, Barnes and Katz sat in a coffee shop. "Another teener," said Katz. "And this one has all the trademarks."

"Gotta be drugs." Agreed Barnes.

"Hey, look." Katz pointed across the square. Back there in the trees. It's the Davis kid."

"Wonder why he's not sitting on the bench with them?"

"Maybe she's the competition."

"Could be," said Barnes. "Maybe we'll be lucky and they'll all kill each other and we can go home. You gonna eat that other donut?"

XXXVI

"It's a hat, looks like."

The deputy sheriff in the green hip waders held up what looked like a waterlogged rag dyed the same color as the swamp by the foul water. The cardboard brim of the cheap gimme hat was as soft as foam rubber under the cloth. The deputy scraped a thumb over the front of the hat and swished it in the water. "Looks like it says Royster Feed and Grain," he said.

"That's where Jack Martin works," said Grover, standing on the water's edge beside Beaudry.

"Or maybe we oughta say worked." Beaudry turned his head in a hundred-eighty degree sweep as if he hoped to see Martin and Tate come trooping out of the moss-hung trees. They had found one of the pair's bear traps chained to a nearby cypress when one of the deputies helping in the search almost stepped in it. They had found another one earlier in the day sprung with a tree branch still stuck in the jaws.

"What do you think?" said Grover.

"I think we're gonna be up to our ass in that muck the rest of the day."

"If they were in there dead, the gators would've eaten them by now."

"But there are some things the gators don't eat. Maybe we'll find one of them. Let's go put on the waders."

XXXVII

"Stand over there by the rock, the one with LSD carved in it." Hannisford peered through the viewfinder of his Nikon lining up his shot. "I'll get a few with both of you in them and then a few with each of you individually." The Knob was a scenic location, but the gray afternoon made the place look grim. It would play well on the page in gritty black and white.

Hannisford had no intention of running any pictures of Jake, but he had to let Jake think he was getting equal billing so that he'd cooperate. Poston was scouting the area around the Knob looking for any sign of the werewolves the boys hadn't seen. If he found some tracks on his own, they wouldn't need Jake at all.

The kid was getting to be a pain in the ass pushing about payment and other issues. The boys gave him an ultimatum when he'd picked them up: cut Roxy out or they wouldn't show him the print they photographed. Roxy's version was more entertaining, and she was much more photogenic than Billy the Kid. The saucer nuts and other faithful readers who bought *Unidentified* would identify with Roxy in a heartbeat.

"Okay, now both of you stand on the rock the monster jumped over. That's it. Point down." Hannisford snapped away. He could just crop Jake out of that one if *Unidentified* decided to use it. He'd get Jake to sign his own release and then say he misrepresented his age and legally couldn't use his picture. Nobody's easier to play than somebody who's so dumb he thinks he's smarter than I am, thought Hannisford. If Roxy played along, he could pull the same stunt with Billy.

Poston came out of the pines behind the boys and walked into the shot. "Elroy, step back about five feet, will you." He'd shoot some pics of him later, crouched down and studying the terrain, and looking like an expert tracker. The magazine would love it.

"Okay, guys, let's go look at the footprint."

"Just so we're clear about this," said Billy. "Roxy's out."

"Maybe we oughta get it in writing," Jake said, looking pointedly at Hannisford.

"Write it down and I'll sign it, okay?" Hannisford looked at the sky. "Make it quick. It looks like it may rain any minute."

Billy and Jake looked at each other. "Uh, do you guys have a paper and pencil?"

"I don't carry a notebook, guys; I use a recorder. This is the only piece of paper I've got. He held up the hundred dollar check. You got a pen, Elroy?"

"Okay, okay," said Jake, realizing he'd pushed too hard. "But Roxy's out of this, right?"

"Sure," said Hannisford. "No Roxy—if the footprint's real, and we can't know that 'til we verify it, can we?"

Jake shrugged and gave a try at an affable grin. "Sure, man, let's go."

"Lead the way."

The trail they followed led down the mountainside from the Knob through stands of bare-limbed trees. Where the forest had looked warm and colorful a week or so before, it now looked cold and menacing, as if something deadly lurked behind every trunk.

Hannisford and Poston lagged behind the boys far enough to talk without being heard.

"Find any tracks up there?"

Poston looked dejected. "Ground's too hard. Too many stones." His disappointment was real; he didn't give a damn about the magazine piece. Poston wanted proof that he wasn't crazy.

"You can find your way back here without them later, can't you?"

"No problem."

"If the track looks good, we can comb over the place without them and maybe find some more. These two aren't woodsmen by a long shot."

Ten minutes later they came to a spot where a small washout crossed the path making the ground softer than the rest of the terrain. "This is it." Jake stood beside a flat rock the size of a dinner plate. He crouched and dug his fingers under the rock and lifted it. "It's still here. Check it out."

Poston and Hannisford hunkered down beside Jake. The impression in the clay may not have been as sharp as the night it was made, but it was clear enough to see its details. The print looked to be basically that of a human foot, large, maybe a size twelve or thirteen. The ball of the foot looked wrong; it was more angular than round. Each of the five toes ended in a deeper hole in the ground. The toes ended in claws.

Hannisford straightened up and unsnapped his camera bag. "I'll get a few shots of the print by itself, then I'll get a few of you guys beside it. Elroy, I want you in the shots too."

Poston didn't seem to hear him. He was staring, transfixed, at the full footprint and comparing it in his mind to a partial he'd seen once before in the Pine Barrens. Poston turned his head and looked at the forest around him. It's out there, he thought. And I'm going to find it.

XXXVIII

The van jolted and bucked along the rutted lane leading to the camp. Maura marveled that they could even drive along what was little more than a trail with ten-inch furrows on either side of a grass-covered hump. Most of the time Slate kept the right wheels on the hump and the left on the edge of the bank. The pine branches and brush scraped the side of the van and Maura would be surprised if there were any paint left on it.

"I guess if you wanted privacy, this is the place to find it," she quipped. "This is wild country. I can't imagine anyone; say a Fuller brush man or a census taker dropping by unannounced."

Slate nodded. "That was a consideration when we set up here. Most of the time when we make a run for supplies or beer we take the airboat."

"How much farther is it?"

"Another half mile, just past that tall stand of pines you see ahead to the right." The van lurched and the steering wheel spun out of Slate's hands for a second. He quickly got control again but not before the van scraped bottom on the hump. He was grateful once again for the steel-plate skid they'd welded under the engine. He blew the horn, one short, one long, two short to let them know it was no enemy approaching.

He rounded the pines and ahead, Maura saw the radio antennas first, then the corrugated tin roof, then the cabin itself and beyond it the dock. Two men were sitting in the shade on the porch. One of them raised a can of beer in an offhand salute. The other stood and started down the steps into the packed dirt of the front yard.

To Maura, they both looked like variations on Slate, not physically; one was taller and lean and the other was shorter and thick like a wrestler, but their bearing tagged them both as Slate's kind, moving with an efficiency that was at once controlled and dangerous.

Slate shut off the motor and climbed out of the van. Haines ambled over as Singer got out of his chair and started down the steps. "Hey, Johnny, glad you're back." He was about to say something else when Maura opened the passenger door and stepped out. "You brought company."

"She's a lot more than that, Mike. Meet Maura Jameson, Ph.D. She's an anthropologist who may be able to help with our 'situation.'"

Haines nodded. "Good to meet you, Doctor Jameson. I'm Mike Haines and this guy," he jerked a thumb over his shoulder, "is Singer." Singer smiled and took off his sunglasses, unabashedly looking her over from head to toe.

"I have a lot to tell you guys about," Slate said. "Where's Swede?"

"We have a few things to tell you too, Johnny. Speak freely?"

Slate looked to Maura and nodded. "She knows the score."

"Things got a little complicated while you were gone."

At that moment the screen door groaned and Swede came outside, his arm in a sling and gauze patches on his chest and shoulder. "What happened?" Slate said.

"Swede had a little run-in with a couple of locals out in the swamp. One of them shot him."

"And the locals?"

Haines made a motion with his two fists like breaking a stick in two, turning both thumbs down.

Slate nodded. "Static?"

"Georgia Patrol came by looking for them today. Nothing to find; Singer saw to that, but I'm guessing they'll be back."

"We'll deal with them if and when. In the meantime, we have other things to think about." He turned to Maura. "Let's go inside. You can wash up a little if you want. I wouldn't advise taking a bath in the lake unless you're good at wrestling alligators, but if you want to use it, there's a camp shower rigged out back. We'll respect your privacy." He said it with absolute gravity.

Maura laughed. "Years of living in the jungle, the desert and the tundra with explorers natives and revolutionaries wore off any modesty I had years ago. Show me the way."

As Slate walked Maura around the cabin, Swede joined Haines and Singer in the yard. "She looks tough," said Singer.

"Agreed," said Haines. "She'd have to be or Johnny wouldn't have brought her out here."

"I trust Johnny. If he trusts her, I trust her," said Singer.

"That's about it," said Swede. "Besides, how many options have we got?"

In a minute, Slate returned. "So, tell me what happened, Swede."

"Two-Zero for the home team." He told Slate about his encounter with the trappers and Singer and Haines jumped in to tell about his rescue and the visit by Beaudry and Grover. By the time they were finished Maura was walking around the corner of the cabin fluffing the last of the water from her hair.

"How much does she know?" said Singer.

"Most of it. As much as she needs to. We can't expect her to help us if she doesn't know what's involved and what danger she's in. She doesn't seem bothered, though. For her, it's all about discovery."

Haines said, "Well, she'll discover more than she bargained for in a few days."

"And in the meantime," Slate said, "we have a lot to do."

XXXIX

"I still don't like it, Jake." Billy frowned.

"Here's the check, man. A hundred bucks. The fat dude said it was okay."

"I still wish we could cash it right now. Man, I hate waiting 'til Monday."

"Maybe we could skip school and be at First National when they open. Then we'll have the cash."

"Yeah, but what about Roxy? All we have is their word that they'll leave her out of the deal. I don't trust those guys, especially that Hannisford, the photographer."

"I know what you mean," Jake said. "I didn't like that other guy, Elroy, either."

"Well, I guess we don't have to like them as long as they're paying us. But I still don't feel right about this deal."

"Relax. One way or the other, we'll get we've got coming."

XL

Robert Mansoor walked out of Lindstrom Hall with no more information about Maura Jameson than he had when he went in. Her office door was locked, and a janitor he bribed with a twenty dollar bill told him that she hadn't been around for days. Maura's red Chevy Nova hadn't moved from its assigned space in the faculty lot. Likewise her apartment; Mansoor wasted an entire frustrating day and night sitting in his old green Pontiac drinking coffee and staring at the building watching for some sign of her. Nothing.

She and Slate had the Devereaux Manuscript, he had no doubt. There was no hue and cry from the library, so that meant Slate had covered the theft well. The question was, why would they run? Had they played him for a fool, or had Slate played both of them? Maura couldn't read the book without a code key, and Slate may have suspected that Mansoor had one, but he didn't know for sure. Did Slate have a key too?

On the surface, Slate needed the book to control his lycanthropy, but did he have greater plans beyond that? Another question stung him: was Maura still alive?

Mansoor slid behind the wheel and started the engine. Slate was a clever and a dangerous adversary; dealing with him would require extreme measures. At that moment, a dark serpent slithered through Mansoor's mind and the Professor decided in order to gain the grimoire, he would take them all.

XLI

Of the four, Singer was the best at breaking codes, and after looking through the grimoire for a few minutes, he said, "Nothing jumps out at me, but I'll give it a shot," and disappeared into the bedroom for quiet and workspace while Haines cooked supper.

By the time they sat down to eat, Singer had a few ideas. "It looks like an alphabet code of some sort, but not like any I've seen before. If the base language is English, it'll be a lot easier. If not, it may take longer to decode, but I haven't seen any symbols in the text that go beyond the twenty-six letters in the English alphabet, and all twenty-six show up." No double vowels or consonants to suggest a foreign alphabet over twenty-six."

"You're translating the whole book?" Maura said.

Singer shook his head. "Not yet. I'm doing the pages before and after the one with the picture of the amulet. What'd you call it?"

"The *farkas ostor.*"

Singer slid a notepad and pencil across the table to her. "Write down the spelling for me. It may help if I can find a six-letter and five-letter word side by side on the page with the picture."

XLII

Poston tired of the Cozy Nook's fuzzy TV reception and left his room. Hannisford was already asleep; he knew because when he turned off the television set he could hear the fat slob snoring like a chainsaw through the thin wall between their rooms. A mile or so toward town was a roadhouse called Leo's, and that was Poston's objective. A two-hour vacation from the quest.

He crouched beside the left front wheel well of Hannisford's Jeep and felt inside the fender for the magnetic box where Hannisford kept his spare set of keys. Poston saw him retrieve it once when he'd locked his keys inside. His fingers closed on the key keeper. The idiot didn't even have the common sense to put it someplace new. In another minute Poston was pulling out of the gravel parking lot.

Leo's looked as if it were designed by the same architect as the Cozy Nook. The walls were cinder block and the roof was flat. Neon beer signs painted the eight or ten cars and pickup trucks out front a rainbow of garish hues. As he got out of the Jeep, Poston heard the thump of the bass notes from the jukebox inside. When he opened the door to step in, the rest of the sound spectrum blasted out; an old Hank Williams tune. It was loud, but at least it wasn't that goddamned psychedelic crap.

Leo's was lit inside like it was lit outside, orange, yellow, purple and blue from the same kinds of signs as the windows. The crowd looked sparse for a Saturday night then Poston remembered that the Chiefs had a football game at Chambliss High School. It likely siphoned away a chunk of the regulars. Some couples lounged in booths along one wall, but most of the patrons were perched on stools. They stared at the stranger in the mirrors behind an impressive line of liquor bottles and Poston returned the favor. They looked away first, and Poston took a stool with an empty one on either side.

The bartender was a surly lout with a bald head and acne scars. He brought Poston a mug of draft and set the shot glass beside it. "One-fifty, bud."

Poston put a five on the bar and stared him down. The bartender took the bill to the register and while he made change, Poston read the back of the T-shirt that bulged with his build: *The Iron Shop-where men are made.* Poston shook his head and knocked back the shot. The whiskey was cheap but it was definitely a hundred proof. As he sipped the beer, the bartender brought his change and set it on the bar. He's one to watch, thought Poston.

The jukebox went quiet for a while but the conversations didn't. Jacked up to compete with the loud music, the barflies didn't seem to notice how loud they were talking.

"Hell, if I was the Sheriff, I'd drag the whole swamp 'til I found those two."

Poston's head raised a little and he turned his head to better hear the conversation. The speaker was a tall, rangy man in a down vest who made the exaggerated sweeping gestures of a drunk as he spoke but somehow managed to not spill a drop of his long-necked Coors. "I heard they found a Royster's Feed cap over in the north marsh. Might be Jack Martin's."

"Or anybody else's who went in the store in the last year," another of the barflies said. "Royster gives those hats out like candy to anybody who comes in. Why do you think they call 'em 'gimme' hats, Bob?"

"I heard they seen a bear out in the woods," another chimed in. "Connor said they were layin' for him, setting traps and all."

"They probably went on a bender and headed to some cathouse in the next county; Maybelles' or The Red Lantern, most likely."

"Then how'd they get there," leered Bob, spreading his arms, "fly? The Patrol found Connor's truck at the edge of the swamp. Jack's truck was parked in front of his house." Bob put his face almost nose to nose to his antagonist and raised his eyebrows."Answer me that one, Mannix."

The bartender came back to Poston. "Hit you again?"

Poston shook his head. "Not yet. You have today's paper?"

The bartender raised one eyebrow and lowered the other in a practiced look of disdain. "This look like a library to you, bud?"

Poston shook his head and set down his mug. "Not even close." He scooped his change off the bar and shoved it into his pocket, including the bartender's tip, stood up, and walked out the door as the jukebox blared anew. He backed the Jeep out of the parking lot and aimed it toward town looking for a newspaper. He found one in an all-night café up the road.

The story was on the second page near the bottom. The headline read: Police Search for Local Men. The article told about the Georgia Patrol combing the area swamps for two missing hunters, Jack Martin, and Connor Tate whose truck had been found abandoned the day before. Something clicked in Poston's head.

He thought about the Tuttle brothers, Danny, Cameron, and Jim, poachers, pot growers and generally bad actors who burned up in a forest fire in the Pine Barrens under suspicious circumstances; the same fire that led to Hannisford catching the werewolf with a trip wire camera. He didn't want to raise his hopes too high, but there might be a connection.

But, he thought, the moon is days from full. It couldn't be the werewolves, yet it still looked too much like the Pine Barrens to be coincidental. Beaudry was the name of the lead officer for the Georgia Patrol. Poston decided to look him up and maybe take a trip to the swamp to look around.

He pulled the Jeep in front of the motel and sat for a while listening to the tick of the cooling engine. He'd like to cut his ties with Hannisford, but that would leave him in the middle of nowhere without a car or a bankroll. Damn. He put the spare key back under the fender, went into his room and stretched out on the lumpy bed.

Sleep was a long time coming, but when it finally did, Poston didn't stir until Hannisford pounded on the door to wake him to go to breakfast.

"After we're done eating, we can go back to the Knob and look for more tracks," Hannisford said. "There have to be more unless the one they showed us was a fake."

"And if it is? You shouldn't have given them the check so fast. Those two are probably laughing their asses off right now at how they fooled you."

"They can laugh today," Hannisford said, waving to the waitress and holding up his coffee mug. "I called the office and they stopped payment on the check Friday."

"What happens when they try to cash it?"

"I'll shrug and say there must be some misunderstanding. I can't have those two making demands about what we do and don't run in the magazine. I have my own pics of the footprint now, so we don't need the ones they sent in; they were crappy Polaroids anyway. We'll go back up there today and look for more evidence. If the story and the print turn out to be bogus, then by the time they get to the bank on Monday, we'll be on the road back to New York."

"Maybe not so soon."

"What are you talking about?"

Poston told Hannisford about the missing hunters. "We need to follow up that angle. The swamp would be an ideal place for a pack of werewolves to hide out. Maybe those hunters had a run-in with them."

"That's a slim chance, and it could take days to check out. My editor is already bitching about my expense account. Monday's it. Back to the Big Apple."

"This could be a break for both of us."

Hannisford smiled indulgently. "You really want to find an honest-to-goodness werewolf, don't you, Elroy?" He shrugged and spread his hands."I admire your dedication, but I have a paycheck to collect and a boss to answer to, and he says time's up."

"Then you'll be driving back by yourself. I'm sticking around."

"If that's what you want to do."

"Just one favor: leave me a camera."

XLIII

Working off and on all night Singer cracked the code to the Deveraux manuscript.

"It was that easy?" said Haines around a mouthful of breakfast.

"It was tough enough," Singer said. "It was a variation of alphabet substitution but with a rotating anchor."

"You'll have to explain that," Maura said.

"You write the standard alphabet on two strips of paper, line them up then move the bottom one way or the other like a slide rule. Say it puts A under D. Every time A appears in a word, you substitute D, E for B, G for C, and so on."

"That's kid stuff," said Swede. "A grade school kid could crack that."

"He could if that's all Deveraux did with it. But after every six words, he changed the substitutions."

"Ouch," said Haines. "How'd you break that?"

"Deveraux limited his substitutions to a set of six. After he ran through them one time, he started again with the first set. It took me a while, but I figured out the pattern. We're dealing with some dangerous shit here if the magic in this book is for real…"

"It is," Maura broke in. "At least Mansoor and the experts at Duke thought so. That's why it was locked away."

Singer nodded. "Given that it is real, he can't take a chance on making a mistake if he uses any of the info in the book."

"Yeah," said Swede. "He might try to make himself invisible and turn himself into a tree or something worse."

"My point exactly," Singer went on. "So he needed a way to keep the rotating codes straight. A six-word sequence, a six-set rotation; I tried his first name, Claude: six letters; no luck, but then I tried his name written backward: E-D-U-A-L-C. Six unique letters. E for A didn't work, but A for E did. If he'd used another six-letter sequence, I might never have broken his code. Numbers helped too. They were all written out as words instead of numerals. All things considered, it's a pretty sophisticated code for a hundred years ago."

"Good thing you know how to read French," said Slate. "That's why we keep you on the payroll."

"Six-six-six," said Maura. "Makes sense; that's the number of the Beast in the Book of Revelation in the Bible."

"I skipped Sunday school and went fishing that morning," said Swede. "What's that all about?"

"The ultimate evil," said Maura. "That's why we can't let the book out of our hands. I suspect that Robert wanted the book for more than just a balance of power. He had ambitions a long way past that. And that's why we only translate the passage on the *farkas ostor*."

"Why?" said Singer.

"The temptation of power is too strong for any of us to resist forever. And the forces that book can unleash demand a price that none of us wants to pay. You've all seen what magic can do. It doesn't work for free."

"You mean like atomic energy." Slate lit a cigarette, blew out a lungful of smoke and continued. "The power's there but there are consequences for using it."

Maura nodded. "Yes; you can't touch it without some taint, and there are responsibilities that go along with it beyond simple self-preservation."

"So we translate the passages about the amulet and stop."

"That would be wise," Maura said, "or there's no telling what might happen." And no one spoke for a long time.

XLIV

Hannisford and Poston spent the gray afternoon combing through the woods and hiking the trail where Billy and Jake had shown them the footprint. Poston had found tracks from deer, rabbits, and even a bobcat, but no match for the track under the rock. If there were others, the weather had erased them.

Hannisford said, "Well, I guess we're not going to find any more tracks out here. Let's get back to the Jeep before it starts to rain."

Poston agreed and the pair started the long trek back to the Knob. "So no tracks means no story?"

"Naah. That rag I work for will publish it; they'll just treat it as an unsubstantiated claim. The readers don't care. They want to be entertained with a good yarn but have the option to believe it or not. Most of them want to believe it's real."

"And you? Do you believe it?"

Hannisford stopped and thought a moment then dropped his wise-guy attitude. He looked Poston in the eye and said, "The werewolves? Who knows? Maybe they are real, maybe not. But the paranormal as a whole? Let's just say I've seen a few things that make me want to not believe." He shuddered at the memory of his encounter with the wizard Pegg in his apartment. "And let's leave it at that." He turned away and started walking again with Poston staring after him.

"Well, I believe it," Poston said. "Because I saw it."

"Yeah," Hannisford said over his shoulder. "You told me that story. I'm sorry my editor didn't want to run it, but the dead guys were shot. Werewolves don't use bullets."

"So you're giving up, just like that?"

Hannisford stopped and turned to face Poston. "Elroy, it's not my call. I'd like to stay here with you in charming Nowhereville and hunt

werewolves forever, but that costs money, and my editor is shutting off the
tap. You get that?"

Poston clenched his jaw and said through his teeth. "Yeah, I get it."
And the pair walked in silence the rest of the way to the Jeep.

XLV

The van bounced the last ten feet and rolled onto the marginally better
gravel road toward Chambliss. Haines drove and Singer slouched in
the passenger seat half asleep, his boonie hat pulled down over his eyes.
Most of the time they could take the airboat to Red's and get whatever
supplies they needed, but some things they could only buy in town; Red's
didn't have a pharmacy department. The full moon was coming, and
everybody was on edge, not knowing how things might develop.

Slate decided that although Singer had translated the passage from the
Deveraux Manuscript, they should wait until the second night of their
turning before letting Maura try her hand at using the amulet. He wanted
to see how she would react to the team in werewolf form before allowing
her to control them in any way. Singer would stop her if he saw she was
doing anything inimical to the team, but at this stage, it was all new. How
could Singer be sure? Another issue: how would the team react to Maura?
Again, Singer would be the control factor.

On another front, the cops; Beaudry and his partner hadn't come back,
which could be good news or bad news. Good news if he decided they had
nothing to do with Martin and Tate's disappearance. Bad news if he was
out there watching them from the shadows, waiting for them to slip. They
would have to leave the camp to turn. The swamp was too risky right now.

Haines pulled to the side of the road to let a rusted pickup truck
rattle past. The man and woman inside stared at them with suspicion
and borderline hostility from the cab. Their heads turned to continue
to stare as they passed, and when Haines raised a hand in greeting, the
expressions didn't change.

Haines looked in the mirror as the truck rattled away and saw two
things; one a gun rack in the back window of the cab with a pair of top
line deer rifles, and the other, three children, none older than eight or
nine years, dressed in little more than rags huddled together in the bed.

They stared back at the van with the same cold, hard eyes as the man and woman in the cab.

"Reminds me of the kids we saw in 'Nam," Haines said.

"No," said Singer. "In 'Nam, the kids' parents gave a damn."

XLVI

Maura sat at the kitchen table in the cabin studying the pages of handwritten text Singer had translated from the grimoire. She knew enough about ritual magic to recognize patterns among the words and the odd syntax. Sorcerers often configured spells in odd word arrangements so that they would be difficult for someone else hearing them to remember and write down later. The odd wording often made the spells difficult for the sorcerer as well, hence the necessity to compile a grimoire. Reciting a spell incorrectly could lead to anything from a simple failure to a cataclysmic disaster, depending on the spell.

The spell to activate the *farkas ostor* comprised only three sentences in the grimoire. The surrounding material, before and after consisted of Deveraux's notes and observations concerning the spell and its use. Devereaux learned the spell as a student of another wizard and when his mentor died, Devereaux inherited the old mage's collection of books and artifacts, including a *farkas ostor*. How many existed in the world Maura had no idea, but she was about to hold one in her hand.

The screen door groaned and Slate came in with a tin box under his arm. He set it on the table and opened the lid. Inside was an object wrapped in a tattered blue rag. Slate looked away as he drew the cloth from the amulet.

Maura stared at the *farkas ostor* for a moment before she took it out of the box. It was as the illustration in the grimoire and Slate's rubbing portrayed it; intertwining silver vines forming a hexagonal shape, inscribed with runes and surrounding a purple gemstone. She held it her palm and felt its weight, not only its physical heft but the weight of the power it represented.

"I've read about this for years. It's hard for me to accept that it's real."

"It was real enough when Pegg used it on me," Slate said. His eye kept drifting toward the stone in the amulet and he had to turn his back to it.

Maura had read opinions from many scholars that magic was not an art but a science; cause and effect. Say the right words, juxtapose the right elements, and you get a specific result. She hoped they were right. She'd reached the juncture where she had to do one thing or the other, and her course was set.

The grimoire mentioned no protective runes, no magic pentagrams to stand in or other necessary safeguards for using the amulet. Just say the words. She took a deep breath and recited the spell.

The gemstone in the *farkas ostor* began to glow and the air seemed to hum in the room. The amulet warmed in her palm, but not hot enough to hurt. Maura felt a faint sensation as if some previously dark niche in her brain lit ever so dimly.

Slate, his back still to the amulet, noticed what felt like wispy tendrils coursing around him, as if trying to find a way into him, under his skin. They passed over in a few seconds and moved on.

"John, are you ready?"

"Yeah, I'm ready."

"Turn around."

Maura held the amulet at face level and Slate stared into the glowing stone at its center. It tugged at his mind, but couldn't seem to quite take hold. "What do you feel?" she said.

"Nothing. At least nothing like when Pegg used it."

"But Pegg used it while you were turning and while you were a werewolf, right?"

"Yeah, never when I was a human."

"And always when the moon was full."

"And risen. Maybe it doesn't work any other time." Slate shook his head to clear it and turned away from the glowing gemstone. "Cover that thing, will you."

"In a minute," Maura said. She recited a few simple words and the glow in the stone faded. Slate looked visibly relieved. "Are you all right, John?"

Slate took a deep breath and clenched and opened his fists a few times. "Yeah, I think so. How about you?"

"I'm okay." She didn't mention the twinge of a headache she felt creeping around the side of her skull. "I'm okay." She wrapped the *farkas ostor* in the blue cloth, put it back into the tin box, and shut the lid. "So far so good."

Slate looked outside through the screen door. "Yeah, the sun's still shining and the birds are still squawking. I guess everything is okay." He picked up the tin box. "I'll put this away for now." He walked out leaving Maura alone.

"Are you all right, John?"

She sat at the table feeling at once the exhilaration that comes with discovery and success, and the fear of opening a new door into a darkened room.

• • •

Greystone had been reading in his room in the farmhouse when the odd twinge struck him like a fly landing on a spider's web. It was faint but undeniable. Unshielded magic. He pondered the ramifications and opened a drawer in his desk. He drew out a thick folded sheet of paper. The wizard spread the Rand McNally map of the United States on his desk. In its margins and corners, runes were drawn in dark ink.

Greystone muttered a few words under his breath, closed his eyes, and put his index finger on the map. Like a planchette on a Ouija board, his fingertip slid across the paper and came to rest. Where magic was, so was power and the means to use it. He was sure that others had noticed as well, and he would have to move quickly to seize it before another like him got to it first.

"Smith." Little more than a murmur, but it brought Mister Smith to the door in seconds.

He bowed deferentially to his master. "Yes, sir?"

"Prepare the car. You are going to Georgia."

"Yes, sir."

XLVII

The van sat at a stoplight, one of three on the main drag of Chambliss. Singer looked to his left and said with a sudden urgency, "Mike. Ten o'clock getting out of the Jeep."

Haines looked across the street and saw a fat guy in a safari vest over a sweatshirt on the street side and caught a glimpse of a guy in denim and a ball cap getting out of the passenger side. The passenger took off his hat and ran a hand over his close-crosspped hair, giving Haines a good look at his face.

"You see the guy in the jean jacket?"

Haines nodded.

"It's him, isn't it?" Singer said. "The Ranger."

"Yeah, I think so."

"What's doing here?"

"Nothing good for us. Let's pick up what we need and get back out to camp."

• • •

"You're sure it was him?" Slate said.

"We didn't ask him for I.D., but I'd say yeah," said Singer.

"Slate went back into the bedroom of the cabin and came back with a thick file folder. He opened it and thumbed through newspaper clippings and notes, past Hannisford's picture of him as a werewolf in the Pine Barrens from the cover of *The Arcane Observer* to a front page newspaper article with a row of photographs; three dead mobsters and the alleged shooter, Park Service Warden Elroy Poston.

The pictures of Michael Monzo's gunmen were mug shots. Poston's was a file photo from his Park Service jacket, which looked oddly similar to the other two pictures. All three were posed against a height grid, all four held an I.D. signboard at chest level, and none of them was smiling. He laid the sheet on the table. "Is that our boy?"

Haines and Singer bent over the picture, studying it. "Yeah, that's him," said Singer. "I'd bet money on it." Haines nodded.

"Who was with him?"

"Some fat guy with glasses."

Slate shook his head. "The photographer." He flipped through the folder and found *The Arcane Observer*. Under the cover photo was the credit "Photograph by William Hannisford." "I remember seeing him in the Pine Barrens."

"So what are they doing here?" said Swede.

"What else?" Slate said. "They're looking for me, just like everybody."

"So what does this mean?" Maura asked.

"It means after the full moon we pull out of here."

"Isn't it dangerous to stay here if people are looking for you?"

"It's more dangerous to turn in a place we don't know. Here, nobody can sneak up on us, we know plenty of places to hide, and this swamp's so big two people couldn't find us in a year even if we stood still."

"I agree with Johnny," said Haines. "We should be okay through the full moon; then we can move to another new hideout."

"I wonder what brought them here?" said Singer.

Slate tapped the *Arcane Observer* photo. "That. Hannisford's a tabloid camera jockey; I'm betting they're here on a tip from someone who's seen us."

"The kids."

"Yeah," said Slate. "The kids."

XLVIII

H annisford pulled into the Cozy Nook and he and Poston headed for his room. "Let's be clear, Elroy. I'm going to leave one of my cameras for you to use but you have to agree that any pictures you take with it that have publication possibility go under my byline and I get the money for them. And if there's any damage to the camera, you're on the hook."

"I get it," said Poston. "I don't give a damn about your byline or the money. I just need the camera."

Hannisford turned the key and found the knob was unlocked. "What the hell?" The door swung open and the pair found themselves facing a badge. Katz stood just inside the doorway. He smiled. "FBI. Come on in, Bill. You too, Elroy. We need to talk."

Poston heard a crunch of gravel behind him and turned to see Barnes, hand inside his suit jacket on the butt of his revolver. Barnes jerked his chin toward the open door, and Poston followed Hannisford into the room.

Hannisford's suitcase lay open on the bed, its contents heaped in it as if someone dumped it out then scooped everything up and threw it back in. His camera bag was on the end table, the top flap open and his film cans lined up like soldiers in parade formation across the nightstand.

"I didn't see much in your camera bag," Katz said with the smug grin cops must practice in the rear view mirror when they're parked in a squad car. "But I found some interesting stuff in your suitcase. He held up a magazine. *Carny Girls.*" He smirked and held up another. "*White Trash Women.* Your literary taste leaves a bit to be desired, Willie Boy."

Hannisford sputtered. "You have no right to come in here like this. You need a warrant."

Katz nodded. "Yeah, I guess so." He spoke over Hannisford's shoulder. "What do you think, Barnes? The Federal Court House in Macon's closed for the weekend. Maybe we could find a judge by tomorrow and if he's not too busy, maybe get him to write us up the paperwork by the next day."

He looked Hannisford in the eye and his smirk turned to a look of pure malice. "And in the meantime, you two would have to wait in this armpit of a room, and to make sure you don't get away, we'd have to cuff you to the radiator, or better yet cuff you two to each other."

Hannisford raised his hands as if Katz had put a gun in his face. "Sure. Go ahead. Tear the place apart. There's nothing to find. I'm a photojournalist on assignment. You're interfering with freedom of the press."

Katz snorted. "Give me a break, fat boy. What are you two really doing down here in the butt end of the universe?"

"We're following a lead."

"You're following a lead." Katz jerked a thumb at Poston. "What's he doing here?"

"He's helping me. He's a specialist. A woodsman."

"Let me get this straight. You're in small town U.S.A. with a man linked to the shooting of three mobsters as part of a purge of the Monzo crime family and their drug operation, and you expect us to believe you're hunting for Bigfoot or something?"

"Actually, it's werewolves."

"Werewolves?" Katz and Barnes laughed. Poston didn't. "That's why you have that trank rifle in your room, Elroy? Yeah, we've been there already. I hope you have a receipt for that night vision scope."

Poston bristled and Barnes said, "Easy, pal." He turned and saw Barnes step back, his .38 halfway out of the holster.

"Let me tell you what I think," Katz said. "I think you two are here setting up some kind of a drug deal and using the local kids, that hippie chick and those two meathead jocks as your runners. And I think you plan on using that rich red Georgia soil to grow weed, just like your buddies in the Barrens, the late Tuttle Brothers." He jabbed a finger at Poston. "You saw what they had going, and you think you can set up that kind of operation here. I think it's all in the same barrel, Elroy."

"The Tuttles died in a forest fire," said Poston.

"Did they die in the fire, or did you set it to burn up evidence that you killed them? Motive plus proximity. I hear two good old boys are missing in the swamp near here. One has to wonder, were they growing weed too, and did they meet the same ignominious end as the Tuttle brothers?"

Poston snarled. "I haven't murdered anybody. I was acquitted."

"Of killing Monzo's boys, but the Tuttle brothers are still an open file. The only reason we're not reading you two clowns your Miranda rights is we didn't find anything worthwhile in your rooms. We'll get a warrant for the Jeep." He leered at Hannisford. "I really want to bust you two; know why? Because of you, I've had to spend the last three days in this god-forsaken town listening to hillbilly music and getting heartburn from chicken fried everything. Like they say in the movies, don't leave town."

"As an extra added attraction," Barnes said, reaching into his suit pocket, "maybe you can tell us about this guy." He unfolded a photocopy of a sketch of a dark-haired man with a beard and a moustache and a scar splitting his eyebrow. He held the sketch up for Poston to study. Poston shook his head. "Never saw him before."

"Thought you might know the man and why the Monzos were looking for him." He showed the picture to Hannisford and caught a flash of recognition in his eyes. It was the same sketch Pegg had shown him in his apartment in Jersey.

"Who is he?" Poston said.

"In case you haven't made his acquaintance, he calls himself John Slate, among other names. Oh, and is it okay to tell him about the werewolves?" Barnes looked to Katz who winked. "They left town a week ago on the last flying saucer for Venus."

Katz and Barnes were still laughing when they left the room without bothering to close the door.

Poston watched through the doorway as they crossed the parking lot to their nondescript undercover car. "Guess you won't be leaving today after all."

XLIX

"Do you really think we'll find something out here?" Grover waved away a swarm of mosquitoes with his hat. "It's been days. If Tate and Martin's bodies were here, the gators would have gotten them by now."

Men, some wearing uniforms and some in hunting clothes under chest waders were dragging poles through the shallow water and poking them into the soft mud beneath. They had spent the most of their Saturday searching the areas near the bear traps Martin and Tate had set. One of the sheriff's deputies sat on the bank with a shotgun watching for gators.

Beaudry shook his head. "No, I don't expect we'll find them, but with an election year coming up when Sheriff Orville Brander makes an official request for help on a weekend afternoon from the Attorney General, who also happens to be his brother-in-law, who's to say no. Why else marry his kid sister?"

"Can't be for her looks," Grover said. "The woman's got a chin like the cowcatcher on a steam engine."

At that moment one of the deputies yelped in pain and everyone jumped. The deputy with the shotgun swung its barrel side to side looking for a target. Clete Johnson, the deputy, was hopping on his right foot. He raised the left out of the water and Beaudry saw the handle of a good sized knife sticking out of the thick green rubber sole of Clete's waders. Johnson held onto his pole with one hand and with the other tugged at the blade with no success.

"God damn it," Clete shouted. "It's a hunting knife. Sumbitch near cut my foot off." He hobbled toward solid ground using the pole as a crutch, but the soft mud made it less than effective. The pole sunk deeper than he expected and he lost his balance, going backward into the foul water.

Clete struggled to his feet to the laughter of the other searchers. He lumbered to the bank glowering at them. "My waders are full of water," he growled. "Somebody gimme a hand." The added weight made it even more difficult for Clete to get out of the mud, so Beaudry and Grover each grabbed an arm and pulled him onto the bank.

Clete sat heavily on a hummock of coarse grass and bent forward. He tugged at the handle of the knife and the blade came free. It was a wicked one, about ten inches from pommel to tip with a clip point blade and a flat crossbar guard. The pommel was a stubby brass cone designed to crack heads. Its blade was heavier than most knives, a quarter inch thick along the back, and Beaudry had no doubt that with it he could hack down a small tree with no trouble, or hack off a man's arm or leg or head. The back was ground with sawtooth serrations like bayonets Beaudry had seen.

"That's a real handful of knife. What's that all about?" said Grover, pointing to the saw teeth.

"In the old days if a soldier was to gig a man with a smooth bayonet, sometimes suction would hold it in and he'd have to fire the weapon to have enough force to pull it out. Those teeth rip up the flesh and let air in around it so you can pull it out without wasting a bullet or making noise."

"Never saw one quite like that before."

"It's a Ka-Bar. Combat knife."

"Them waders is almost new," Clete grumbled, dumping the water out of one leg then the other. "Who's gonna pay for them?" He pushed an arm into the damaged leg and poked a finger through the gash the knife had left in the rubber. "Damn it." His left foot was bleeding steadily from a slash inside the arch. "Somebody better drive me to the hospital for a tetanus shot before I die of the lockjaw."

Beaudry ran his thumb over the knife's edge. He drew it across a strap of the wader and the Ka-Bar parted the thick rubber as slick as a razor blade. "Grover, I think it's time we go back to the Parker place and talk to those vets."

As they climbed into their patrol car, Clete yelled after them, "Hey! Where you going? Who's gonna drive me to the doctor?"

"Try pissing on it," said Grover. "Worked for my granddaddy and he lived to be ninety."

As he drove away, Beaudry saw Clete give them the finger in his rear view mirror.

"You never did tell me if you followed up on that airboat," Beaudry said.

"Belongs to a fellow named Hicks lives in Pottstown up in Lumpkin County."

"Not one of them, huh?"

"Nope. Hicks says they rented it from him; paid him for six months in advance in cash."

"Who paid him?"

"He says Crawford, the slick one did most of the talking and signed the paperwork. Hicks is happy about it. Says he's got Parkinson's Disease and can't use it himself anymore. He's hoping they'll buy it from him."

Beaudry nodded. "Maybe he'll hit it lucky and they'll do that. Of course maybe, he's hit it lucky already."

"What do you mean?"

Beaudry looked at the knife in the evidence bag on the seat between them. "I mean he may be lucky they didn't just take the airboat and use that knife to cut his throat."

L

Billy was on patrol in his father's Bonneville. He was cruising the streets of Chambliss looking for Roxy. When he called the house, her mother said she had gone for a walk, so he begged the car from his dad and set out on a search. Better to talk to her in person than over the phone, he thought. She can't hang up on me before we get some things settled.

Roxy was a block away from the park when Billy caught up with her. She wore her bell-bottomed jeans and some kind of khaki Army shirt with epaulets. Her dark frizzy hair was pulled into a ponytail that exploded out of the rubber band like a pom-pom. He pulled alongside her in the Bonneville and rolled down the window. "Hey, Roxy, need a ride?" She ignored him and kept walking. "Aw, come on. Don't be that way. Get in. I'll take you home."

She stopped and turned to face him. She was wearing regular glasses today, not her little square granny shades and the look in her eyes withered his smile a little. "I'm not going home right now," she said in a voice that could turn alcohol into ice cubes. "And I don't want to get in. I'm not going anywhere with you."

"Look, Roxy, I just want to talk."

"I'll bet you do. I heard the version of the werewolf story you told those men from *Unidentified*. You the big brave hero chasing the monsters away with your little ball bat."

"Hey, I didn't say that."

Roxy's voice was rising and some people in the park, a family with a couple of kids and some teens who knew them both had stopped what they were doing and were paying attention."Something else you didn't say? You didn't even mention my name to them, did you? You just said 'my date.' Not 'my girlfriend' or even 'my friend.' Were you so afraid that somebody might find out you went out with me that you wouldn't even tell them my name?" She was shouting now."And did you tell them you peed your pants?"

Billy's mouth opened and closed a few times but nothing came out. Roxy gave him a hateful glare then turned and started walking fast. He tried to keep up with her, but she stepped off the sidewalk and cut into the park where he couldn't take the car. "Hey, Roxy, come back." She kept moving and didn't look back. Not exactly hanging up on him, but the result was pretty much the same.

Billy stared after her. She was going to screw up everything. He stepped on the gas, squealing his tires and wheeled the big Bonneville around the square and away from the park and the stares of the onlookers. She was going to make him the laughingstock of Chambliss. Jake. Jake would know what to do about her. As he roared away from the town square, he wished he could just make Roxy disappear.

LI

"I never would never have pegged you for a two-pack-a-day smoker," said Singer to Maura. The two sat at the rough wooden table on the porch of the cabin. It was Swede's turn to cook now that his shoulder was healing, and the aroma of venison stew drifted through the screen door.

"When you leave civilization behind, you usually have to park your vices too. I've had to go for months at a time to places where all you have is what you bring with you. Might as well be on the Moon or at the bottom of the ocean. You can only carry so much, so you choose; food or cigarettes, whiskey or a medical kit."

"Sometimes whiskey *is* the medical kit."

They both laughed and Maura went on. "I do without cigarettes the whole time I'm gone, but as soon as I get back, I make up for it because I know I'll be doing without them again before too long. Eat, smoke and be merry, right?"

"We've all been there. What did Johnny tell you about us?"

"That you're professionals."

"You're too polite." Singer gave her a smile. "Call us what we are. We're mercs, mercenaries. That bother you?"

"Not much after living with people in Kazakhstan who play polo with their enemies' heads. I'm guessing you've seen worse."

"I suppose we've all seen the dark side of humanity. Difference is, we're part of it, you aren't."

"I guess I am now," she said, her eyes drifting over the lake. Neither spoke for a long time. Finally, Maura broke the silence. "You're the one they didn't turn, why you?"

"Johnny has his reasons. I'm the Renfield."

Maura chuckled. *"Apropos."* "We were all going to turn, but Johnny thought one of us should still look like his driver's license when the moon was up, just in case."

"And automatic weapons aren't designed for paws and claws."

Singer nodded. "Maybe I'll turn later, depending . . ."

Maura let it go, but from that moment understood that she was being weighed and measured, and wondered what her fate may be if she were found lacking.

Ducks flew over and settled on the water. Singer gestured with his beer can. "Tomorrow's supper, a flock of ducks."

"A badelynge."

"A what?"

"A badelynge. A fancy word for a flock of ducks, like a covey of quail or a gaggle of geese."

Singer laughed. "That's good." He raised his can in a salute. "Here's to education." He took a swig of his beer and said, "What do you call a gang of werewolves?"

Maura's brow folded into a fine set of thought lines. "You call a group of wolves a fleet."

"Sounds too much like the Navy."

"Then I guess you should call it a pack."

Singer nodded. "I like Johnny's name for us: Hitwolf."

Maura let the word sink in, recognizing the camaraderie in Singer's voice. He was not a werewolf himself, but he was part of the team. "Again, *apropos.*"

Then they heard the Georgia Patrol cruiser coming up the lane.

"Johnny," Singer called over his shoulder. "We got company."

Slate came onto the porch, saw the patrol car coming and went quickly inside, returning just as quickly to stand beside Singer and pass something to him. Slate's body blocked the move from view by the officers, but Maura saw what Slate handed Singer, a pistol. Singer tucked it under his shirt and Slate moved away to take a seat at the table.

Beaudry and Grover got out of the car, and Maura could feel the tension in the air. The patrolmen both still wore their mirrored aviator shades though the late day sun was below the tops of the trees. Men with no eyes, thought Maura, but she knew the eyes behind those glasses missed nothing. Beaudry had something wrapped in plastic in his hand that she couldn't make out. She saw the strap over his service revolver was unsnapped and was sure Slate and Singer noticed it too.

He climbed the first two steps onto the porch but Grover hung back to the side. Smart, thought Maura; spreading the targets. Beaudry smiled, showing just the edges of his teeth, but Maura could see by his posture and movement he was as taut as a coiled spring. "Afternoon fellows." He tipped his head but not his hat at Maura, keeping his right hand free. "Ma'am."

Singer raised his beer and nodded. "Officer—Beaudry is it?"

"Yes, sir. Who are your friends?"

"The lady is Penny Winters, and the gentleman is Jim Burns. Did you find your missing hunters?"

Beaudry shook his head. "Not yet, but we did find something unusual." He stepped the rest of the way on the porch and as he did, he took the plastic away from the Ka-Bar and set it on the table in front of them. Maura noticed that he didn't drop it or thump it down emphatically, he treated it as if it were made of glass. He treated it like evidence.

"Like I said, I never made it over, but you fellows have been. I thought maybe you could tell me something about this knife. It's not the usual thing folks carry around here."

"It's a Ka-Bar," said Singer. "Right, Jim?"

Slate picked the knife up by its handle and turned it over side to side. "Yeah, I saw a lot of them in 'Nam, but this one's been altered. The top of the clip's been sharpened, and those saw teeth aren't part of the original design. Where'd you find this?"

"A couple of miles from here in the swamp. We were dragging for bodies and it turned up."

A *Playboy* magazine lay on the table. Slate drew the blade across the cover. It slit the paper cleanly, diagonally severing the Playmate's head from her shoulders. "Sharp enough. Somebody knows how to do it." He handed the knife back to Beaudry, offering it to his right hand. Beaudry reached across his belt buckle and took it with his left and set it on the table.

"Where're your other two friends? Crawford and the big guy?"

"Crawford took the van to Atlanta," Singer said. "Haggerty's inside cooking supper. He makes a pretty good stew. Stick around if you're hungry." He turned his head to the doorway. "Hey, Ray. How long 'til the chow's ready?"

Swede's voice sounded from inside. "About five minutes. Keep your shirt on."

Beaudry could see through the screen door into the cabin. No one was standing at the stove. His scalp tingled and his MP instinct told him a rifle was pointed at his head or Grover's from inside the cabin. "Thanks for the invitation, but we have to get going. Ma'am." He tipped his head to Maura and picked up the Ka-Bar in the plastic sheet with his left hand. As he turned away from the table and climbed down the steps toward the car, Grover stood still, watching. Maura saw his hand dangling just close enough to his holster.

Beaudry and Grover climbed into the cruiser and in a moment they were gone.

Maura let out a long breath. "That was tense."

"They know," said Singer.

"No, they don't, but they suspect." Slate pulled his automatic from his waistband and set it on the table. "If they knew, they would have brought a whole lot more men with them."

"He wanted your fingerprints, didn't he?" Maura said.

"He won't get any from that checkered handle. I was careful to not touch the blade."

Swede stepped out onto the porch with an M-16 under his arm. "Sorry, I got us into this."

Slate shrugged. "*Caca pasa.* We just deal with it. When Haines gets back, we'll have to make some hard decisions about hanging around here."

"Damn," said Singer, and I was just getting used to the place."

"You would have killed them, wouldn't you?" Maura's question was aimed at Slate but took in the whole group.

"Only if they pulled on us first."

Maura was silent for a moment, letting it sink in then she turned to Singer and gave him the fish eye. "Penny Winters? Jesus Christ."

• • •

Beaudry and Grover were silent as they pulled away from the camp. Beaudry's eye kept drifting to the rear view mirror, watching for he didn't know what. Grover, taking the hint, turned it so that he could keep an eye on the receding camp as they bounced down the rutted lane. "You watch the road, Alan. I'll watch our sixes."

"What do you think, Tom?"

"I don't know whether one of them might've killed Martin and Connor, but there's something wrong with that gang. I've seen a lot of hard characters, but nothing quite like them."

"Once, at Pendleton, a squad of what the Major called "specialists" came to the base for a week to train some people in jungle weapons and tactics. They had beards and mustaches covering most of their faces and wore fatigues with no insignia or rank on them.

"I ran into them at the Non Com's club and we bought each other beers. They didn't say much about themselves; maybe they couldn't. They were friendly enough, but when you looked in their eyes, there was nothing inside.

"One of our guys across the room took a picture of somebody else but the Specs were in the background, and one of them got up from his stool, walked over as if he were strolling through the park on a summer day and took the camera right out of the guy's hand. He pulled out the film then handed the camera back to him without a word. The man with the camera opened his mouth to say something, but the Spec said something to him none of us could hear and walked back to his stool. The camera man turned pale and walked out of the club.

"You felt while you were shaking their hands they were sizing you up and figuring what it would take to kill you and whether they wanted to. That's how I felt with those men at the camp. And the woman? Who knows what she's doing there."

"You want to get a warrant?"

Beaudry shook his head. "Not yet. If there was anything to find, it was gone ten minutes after we left the first time. Something funny's going on there, maybe drugs, maybe organized crime, maybe some underground resistance bunch like the Weathermen, but we aren't going to find out coming at them head on. Let's get that knife on its way to the lab and talk to the Lieutenant. We need some strategy."

LII

Haines waited in the twilight, watching the wind blow a few flakes of November snow around the empty roof level of the parking garage. He'd shut the van's motor off a half hour before and could see his breath. He didn't mind the cold; he saw it as a relief from the humid Georgia warmth that clung to him like insulated long johns. He looked at his watch. Parker was officially late as of two minutes ago.

In the near distance, the D.C. monuments glowed, testimony to America's greatness. Tombstones is more like it, Haines thought, shaking a Camel from the pack. He thought of a line from a movie he saw a few months ago: "You know, this used to be a helluva good country." Now it's just one more snake pit full of people who'd sell their mothers to hold onto power.

Haines pushed in the dashboard cigarette lighter. Never waste a match. Old habits. He pressed the tip of the Camel into the orange circle and pulled in a lungful of smoke. At the end of the roof, Haines saw headlights coming up the ramp. It was a Ford, green, nondescript, hubcaps not wheel covers, and black wall tires; a Company fleet vehicle. He reached for the automatic on the seat beside him and waited until the car came close enough that he could see the driver. Heavy horn-rimmed glasses, a mustache like a Fuller brush and a shiny bald head. It was Parker.

Haines waited until Parker stopped the car then started the engine of the van, letting it idle. Parker stepped out of his car leaving the Ford's headlights on, the engine running, and the door open.

"Kill the lights," Haines said, through the window. Parker did and Haines opened the door of the van and slid from the driver's seat, tucking the .45 into his waistband.

Parker was tall and gangly, his tan camel hair topcoat hanging just to his knee where it would hit the shin of a shorter man. "Never thought I'd see you again."

Haines shrugged. "You and lots of other people." He took a drag on his cigarette and let the smoke dribble out of the corners of his mouth.

"You really shouldn't smoke those things. They're bad for you. At least switch to filters."

"Lung cancer is the least of my worries, Parker." Haines reached into his jacket and handed a wad of bills, a fifty on top, to him. Parker looked at the bundle of money through the bottom of his trifocals and drew his thumb across the edge. He smiled. "Looks right." He reached into his topcoat and drew out an envelope. Haines took it without looking at it and slid it into his jacket.

"They're really hot to take you guys off the board. You know that, don't you? You should have stayed in Asia."

"You know better, Parker. Forget you ever saw me."

"Out of sight, out of mind, I always…"

The scrape of metal on concrete made Haines turn and drop as the flat snap of a silenced gun sounded to his left. Parker fell backward clutching his chest and slumped to the concrete against the Ford.

Haines rolled under the car as a second shot ricocheted off the concrete. Haines spotted the hitter, head and shoulders and a long barrel over the rim of the concrete wall. Must be a human fly, thought Haines. He snapped off two shots more to make the sniper duck more than anything, crouched behind the open door and slithered into the Ford, staying below the dash.

The car was aimed in the right general direction. Haines slumped behind the wheel and in one coordinated move yanked the gearshift into Drive, pulled on the headlights and floored the accelerator. Shots spidered the windshield and zinged off the hood and roof as the shooter fired blindly into the headlights, but Haines risked raising his head for a quick look.

The big V8 engine roared and the tires smoked as the Ford hurtled across the roof. A second before impact he saw the wide eyes and open red mouth of the man in the ski mask like a blackface comedian in a minstrel show. The crash wasn't enough to push the car through the wall, but it knocked the shooter from his perch and the minstrel's face disappeared from view. Haines sat behind the wheel and shook his head to clear it.

He lurched out of the Ford, reeling from the crash and hunched low as he ran for the van, expecting a bullet to rip through him any second. He pulled the van in gear and as he drove away, a shot blew out one of the back door windows. In the rear view mirror, Haines saw a man firing a rifle from the open trunk of the Ford. He two wheeled the van onto the exit ramp and sped down and across the next floor of the garage. From the corner of his eye, Haines saw something that made him slam on the brakes.

The hitter in the ski mask was dangling from a line around his waist hanging in the open space between the floors. He was bent half backward at a forty-five-degree angle, his rifle hanging from his left arm where he'd wrapped the sling around it. His eyes were open but if they saw anything it was the gates of Hell.

Haines floored the van and in two minutes, he was heading for the Beltway.

LIII

Three hours later, the second shooter, whose name was Kendry, sat shackled to a chair in a windowless room in Langley. A red lump on his forehead was turning purple. He'd come in expecting a standard debriefing and found himself in custody.

Tom MacDonald sat across a narrow table from him, fingers laced over a yellow notepad with a half page of scribbled notes. "Walk us through it one more time, Kendry. There has to be more to it."

"No, man, I'm telling you. Parker called us in; I mean he has the authority, right? He said he needed us to help him take down a rogue agent. Travis set up on the wall and I hid in the trunk of the car. Travis was supposed to disable him and I was there for backup in case something went wrong."

"Well, it went pretty damned wrong, didn't it?" MacDonald threw his pen on the table in disgust. "Parker's dead, Travis is dead, and the target's in the wind."

"I was in the trunk. I couldn't see anything."

"And when the car took off, why didn't you shoot through the back seat?"

"Hell, I thought Parker was driving the car then when it hit, the impact half knocked me out." He touched the lump on his forehead. "By the time I came to and got the latch open, the guy was driving away."

MacDonald reached into the pocket of his jacket and pulled out four photographs. He laid them face up in front of Kendry, each in its turn, like a dealer in a casino. "Was it one of these men?"

"I don't know I..."

"Look at the pictures, Kendry," MacDonald snapped. "Was it one of them?"

"I told you. I was in the trunk. By the time I got out for a shot, all I saw was the back of the van."

"But you hit the van."

"Hell, yes, I hit the van. I blew out a back window. He kept on going, so I guess I didn't hit the driver."

Someone knocked at the door of the interrogation room. The other agent with MacDonald opened it and Briggs came in. He ignored Kendry and turned to MacDonald. "Anything?"

MacDonald shook his head. "Apparently, Parker was running his own show here. Who knows why, Briggs. Maybe the wad of cash we found beside his body had something to do with it."

"You're Briggs?" said Kendry. "Parker said you authorized this operation."

Briggs stared at Kendry as if he were some exotic species of insect. "Apparently, Parker lied to you." Briggs started out the door. MacDonald scooped up the photos of Slate and his crew and picked up his notepad. Briggs was waiting in the hallway.

"What the hell was Parker doing?" Briggs stood arms akimbo like a petulant child. At that moment, MacDonald wanted to punch him in the face.

"I don't know. We aren't sure whether it even was Slate or any of his people. It's a damned good thing the District cops recognized the license number as one of our cars and phoned us first. The press would be crawling all over us by now otherwise."

"Did you find anything in his office?"

"No, but in his apartment, I found this." Mac held out a charred scrap of paper.

Briggs turned it over in his fingers. "That's the first half of my home address. How did he get it?"

"No great feat. After all, we're in the information business."

The other agent stepped out of the interrogation room and called to Briggs. He asked a question MacDonald couldn't hear, and Briggs said, "He's a liability. Take him out of here and terminate him," and walked away without looking back.

LIV

"Was it one of them?"

Haines stayed on back roads and didn't stop 'til North Carolina where he pulled into the parking lot of a café. He rolled lights off behind the line of trucks looking for what he needed. A big flatbed trailer had machinery wrapped in heavy plastic sheeting. He cut a rectangle from one of the sheets and taped it over the shattered back window with electrician's tape from the toolbox in the van. Next, he switched license plates with a similar van parked nearby. Haines was hungry and the smell of home cooking from the diner was a temptation, but as soon as he tightened the last screw, he was back on the road.

Parker was most likely working on his own dime; otherwise, there would have been more men and better planning. This screw-up was done on the cheap and by the seat of his pants, which is why it was a screw-up. He pulled the envelope from his jacket and slit the flap with his thumbnail.

Inside it, he found three photographs of a house, one including a sandy-haired man in his bathrobe at the front door retrieving a newspaper; a street map of Fairfax, Virginia and a sheet of typewritten paper. Haines read it by the dashboard light. A name: Carlton Briggs and an address. Haines' brow creased in puzzlement. He knew the name. Briggs came on board just before they left for the mission to Laos, although they'd never met him. Maybe Parker was on the level after all and knew nothing about the shooters.

No, that can't be right, he thought. If this were a Company operation, I'd've never driven out of that garage. This was a half-assed spur-of-the-moment deal. But if Parker was selling me out, why not just give me a blank sheet of paper in the envelope. Then it hit Haines. Parker wants Briggs dead as much as we do. The shooters may have been just Parker covering his ass, waiting to see how things shook out. But if so, why did the sniper open fire?

No matter. It's over now. No use second guessing. There's no police chatter on the scanner mounted under the dash. I'd know by now if somebody was tailing me, he thought, and the Company sure as hell wouldn't call the cops to put up roadblocks. That would shine a bright light on the whole SNAFU. And they do like to stay in the shadows.

He switched on the mobile shortwave unit mounted under the dashboard. As it warmed up, he checked the frequency on the dial. The needle was five notches lower than the call frequency he'd be using; never leave the radio on the hot channel—old habits. The radio hummed into life and Haines turned the dial through static and squelch. He keyed the microphone to talk. "Runner to Base, over."

On the third try, he got a response. Singer was monitoring the radio. "Read you, Runner, over."

"Weather?"

"Or not." The joke was Singer's password.

"*Il fait accompli, mon ami.*"

"*C'est ci bon.*"

"Over and out." Haines switched off the radio. Details were for face-to-face, not the airwaves.

He checked his cigarettes. He still had half a pack. If he was lucky they'd last him the rest of the drive.

LV

Maura stood naked on a wide flat rock surrounded by the opaque water of the swamp. It was night but she could see as if it were noon because the full moon was clearing the trees and shining through a gauzy haze of fog that hung over the water. She heard a splash behind her but when she turned, she saw nothing.

A splash to her left then one to her right. In the pale glow, she saw the chevron ripples of snakes swimming toward her, six of them converging on the rock. They slithered from the water and surrounded her, impossibly long, their wet scales shining like droplets of silver. They formed a rough circle then twisted themselves over and under each other into a rough hexagon. The stone beneath her feet began to glow a deep violet.

Runes emerged like red fire on the serpents' skin, and one rose from the group like a cobra, its flat head bobbing, its tongue tasting the air for her scent and smelling terror. The serpent opened its mouth to bare a set of curved fangs as long as her index finger. She saw herself mirrored in the black diamonds of its pupils as it reared back to strike.

• • •

Maura started awake sweating from the nightmare. She stared at the ceiling of the cabin listening to the rain pattering on the tin roof mixed with the snores of the men. She shifted on the cot, and the canvas creaked under her weight. Maura never felt fear, no matter what danger her research and travels put her in, but this time she felt anxiety alongside excited anticipation. She was about to see her research and her beliefs become real.

From what Slate told her about the people pursuing them, she realized that although she had the most amazing story to tell, she couldn't share it with the world. She would be putting them in danger and herself as well. From everything she'd seen of the CIA in faraway places, she understood that people were sources of information to them and little else. They wanted Slate, and if they thought she knew how to find him, her life would be over.

In the distance, Maura heard the sound of an engine approaching. She sat up on the cot and reached for Slate then hesitated, afraid to touch him for fear of how he might react. Instead, she said softly but urgently, "John, wake up." One second Slate was asleep on his back and the next he was sitting up on the cot without making a sound.

"Someone's coming."

Slate leaned forward, listening. "It's the van. Haines is back."

Slate made coffee while Haines told his story about the parking garage ambush. "The question is," said Haines, "is the intel straight on Briggs?"

"Parker understood that if he tried to scam you, he was a dead man, so he couldn't risk giving you a blank sheet of paper. If you opened the envelope, the game was over unless the info looked good."

Haines nodded. "As soon as I handed off the money, the gunplay started. Maybe Parker gave some signal I missed to the sniper."

"Or the shooter thought if he took both of you out he could grab the cash and make a clean getaway. Twenty grand's tempting enough to sell out your boss." Slate shrugged. "It was enough for Parker to sell out his."

"And the man in the trunk?"

"In on it or not, it doesn't matter. They split the cash two ways or the sniper shoots his partner and grabs it all."

"It gives me a headache thinking about it."

"But that's the way they operate, Mike; wheels within wheels."

"Let's say Parker was on the level and the other guys were selling him out. It's the straight dope. Do we go after Briggs and settle the score?"

Slate shook his head. "We don't kill Briggs before we make him tell us whether anyone else was in on it. Briggs takes his orders from somebody higher up like they all do. Killing him might just be like taking an aspirin for cancer. It kills the pain but the source is still there."

"How high do we go?"

"The White House if it's righteous."

Haines stared into his coffee cup. "That's the catch, Johnny. How do we know?"

"We trust our gut. And all those useful interrogation skills the Company taught us. Let's see what Briggs has to say about it."

In the next room, Maura stared at the ceiling, hearing every word. Cold sweat dripped from her forehead onto the rough canvas of the cot. She wouldn't be sleeping anymore tonight.

LVI

The Cadillac sedan rolled quietly through the darkened streets of Chambliss. Mister Smith leisurely turned the steering wheel with one finger and circled the Confederate statue. The headlights swept the storefronts of the town square and the trees of the park. "A charming haystack," Smith said aloud to no one. "Now to find the needle."

There had been no further disturbance in the web of magic since Greystone had detected the unshielded spell, but eventually it would happen again, and when it did, Mister Smith would find its source.

Mister Smith began whistling "Londonderry Air" as he drove from the town square and his taillights disappeared into the night.

LVII

The team sat around the table, breakfast done. Maura stood at the doorway smoking a cigarette and listening.

"So what's the deal, Johnny?" said Swede. "Do we pull out or stay?"

"If we stay, we have the Georgia Patrol keeping an eye on us, and if we take off, we look like we're guilty of something and they'll have an APB out in five minutes. Having Poston, the park ranger in town complicates things."

"He hasn't seen any of us yet," said Haines.

"I think you're right about that," Slate said. "If he had, he might not even recognize us anyway. But he's another hole in the floor to step around."

Singer spoke up. "What about the photographer? Maybe we should shake him down and find out why they're here. He'd be easier to crack than Poston."

"That may be a good idea. If the kids told him about us and he runs the story in some tabloid, we'll have to bail out of here before the swamp turns into the Pine Barrens all over again."

"Okay, Johnny, but that may take a while before he gets that far. We all agree then that we'll have to leave here." Nods around the table. "The question is how soon. Do we wait 'til after the full moon?"

"I don't want to be traveling when we're turning if we can avoid it. Tonight's the full moon. Maybe the best we can do is stay here through tomorrow night and see how Maura," he nodded toward the doorway, "does with the amulet. If it works for her like it did for Pegg, it won't matter where we are when we turn. We can stay out of sight one more time; the swamp's a big enough place to hide in. We get past tonight then we'll decide when to bail. In the meantime, start packing for the move."

"What if Beaudry comes back with an army?"

Swede snorted. "Then he'd better bring a big one."

Slate looked out the screen door past Maura. "From what I've seen of Beaudry and his partner, I'd say they'll bring whatever they need."

"What about the van?" said Haines. "The missing back window makes it easier to spot if the cops are looking. Do we steal a new one?"

"If we're going to leave tomorrow, we may not have time to do that, and we sure as hell won't have time to refit it. But you're right about the back window. There has to be an auto glass repair or a body shop in a town the size of Chambliss. Poston has never seen me—as a human, that is. I'll take it and while I'm in town, I'll see if I can find our boy Hannisford."

Haines said, "In the meantime, we can break down the equipment we need to carry." He threw the keys to Slate.

"How about I take it?" Maura stubbed out her cigarette. "I won't be much use sitting around here."

Slate thought it over and said, "Makes sense." He handed the keys to her. He crossed the kitchen and took the coffee can from the cupboard. He dumped half into a bowl and rooted around in the rest until he found a thick roll of bills. He peeled off a half dozen twenties and handed them to Maura. That should take care of it."

She tucked the money in her jeans. "I'll be back as fast as I can."

As the van rumbled down the lane away from the cabin, Haines said,

"You trust her, John?"

"I trust her obsession. She'll be back. She doesn't want to miss the show."

LVIII

Ross Glass fronted on an alley two blocks from the town square. It was Sunday and the shop was closed, but the owner lived in the back of the building. He assured Maura (with the incentive of an extra twenty bucks) that the window would be finished before lunch time. That left her an hour or so to kill, and she decided to take a walk around Chambliss and see what the town was like. She already ate breakfast, but another cup of coffee was always a good idea. She found a small coffee shop on the town square that looked past the soldier statue to a small park.

Maura ordered coffee and as an afterthought an orange Danish, another guilty pleasure unavailable in the field. She sat at a table by the window and picked up the local weekly newspaper from a nearby table. Antiwar protestors accused the Nixon Administration and the FBI of using AP and UPI crowd photos from the October Moratorium demonstrations to identify protestors as "dissidents" and "dangerous radicals." Maura had participated in one of the demonstrations at Manville, but all she and some of her students did was sing a few songs and chant "Hell no, we won't go." But if the FBI had her on film, so what.

In California, UCLA, and the Stanford Research Institute established their first permanent link in a computer resource-sharing system called the Advanced Research Projects Agency Network in conjunction with the Department of Defense. Called ARPANET, the system was expected to ultimately provide independent communication in times of national emergency. Another colossal waste of taxpayer money,thought Maura. They'd do better to spend it on cancer research.

At the bottom of the front page was a short piece about the missing hunters with a photograph of a search party, men in hunting clothes fanned out across a field with Sheriff Orville Brander in the foreground. Maura felt a cold breath at her neck when she read a statement by the Sheriff: "We are sparing no expense or effort to find these men and we're grateful for the help of the community and the Georgia Patrol." They won't let it go, Maura thought. This isn't good.

The spring bell over the coffee shop door chimed and two men came in. Maura looked up from the newspaper and recognized Elroy Poston from the photo Slate had shown them. The other man, the fat guy with glasses must be the photographer, Hannisford, she thought. They took a table away from the window and she strained to hear their conversation but could hear only bits and snatches over the radio playing behind the counter. Three Dog Night harmonized over One being the loneliest number.

She took the last bite of her pastry, downed her coffee and folded the newspaper. She got up from the table and as she did, Hannisford gave her a once-over that made her skin crawl. He not only undressed her with his eyes, he tied her wrists and ankles to the bedposts and settled in for the night. The photographer gave her a leering grin. Any other day, she would have put him in his place for his pig behavior, but today, she couldn't afford to call attention to herself, especially with these two.

Maura turned her back on them, and in the reflection in the coffee shop's door, she could see Hannisford. His thumbs and forefingers formed a squared-off horseshoe framing her ass as she stepped as stiffly as possible onto the sidewalk.

"She was a good looking piece, wasn't she?" Hannisford said, still leering as he watched Maura pass by the shop window. "I usually go for blondes, but she's got a tight body in those jeans. I'd say she's my type."

"Your type is any woman who'd say yes to you for less than fifty bucks," Poston snorted, "and they're getting to be a rare species." He set down his coffee mug and pointed a finger at Hannisford's face. "We have an opportunity. We can't leave town no matter what tantrum your boss throws, so I say we make the most of it."

"And do what? We've already combed through the area where the kids said they saw the werewolves and didn't find squat. You may want to go wading in that god damned swamp up to your oxters in gators and water moccasins, but not me."

Poston gave Hannisford a contemptuous look. He rose and picked up the newspaper from the table where Maura left it. Poston leafed through it to a back page. A four column block at the bottom was titled "Almanac." He set the paper between Hannisford and his donuts and jabbed a finger at it.

"See that?" Poston pointed to the bottom of the page where shaded diagrams marked the phases of the moon. "The full moon's tonight.

You don't find werewolves in the middle of the afternoon, you find them tonight, and the next night, and the next night."

Hannisford looked up from the paper. "Okay, Elroy, you've talked me into it. We'll go on werewolf watch, but we're going to do it the smart way. I caught that one in the Pine Barrens with a trip wire camera before. Why mess with success? I can set up four cameras. You pick the spots and we'll see what we catch. After all, like you said, we have tonight and tomorrow and tomorrow." He pushed the newspaper aside. "Now let me eat my breakfast in peace."

Maura crossed the square and headed into the park. What a creepy bastard that Hannisford was. She decided that nothing that could happen to him was less than he deserved and she almost wished he would find the werewolves he was looking for. Once would be enough.

When she rounded the corner to Ross glass, she saw the van parked in the little gravel parking lot beside the shop. The window was done already. Inside the owner handed her a bill and she handed him two twenties. "Keep the change," Maura said.

"Keys are under the mat."

"Thanks." She stepped into the pale sunlight and as she reached for the door handle of the van, a hard hand clamped over her wrist. "Maura!" Mansoor loomed over her.

"What do you think you're doing?" Mansoor's eyes were wild. He looked as if he hadn't slept and had the facial tics of somebody running on bennies. "You can't use unshielded spells without people noticing. If I found you, so will he."

Maura twisted in Mansoor's grip but couldn't break free. "Who? Who will find me?"

"Greystone. He wants the *farkas ostor*, and if he learns you have the Deveraux grimoire, he'll do anything to get it, and he mustn't have it."

Her eyes blazed with anger. "And you must? I may not know everything about magic, but I know enough not to let you have it either."

"No, no, you've got to give it to me."

"Or what?" Maura's eyes darted back and forth looking for anyone she could call out to for help, but the alley was empty.

Mansoor grabbed a handful of her hair with his free hand and yanked her head back. "There is no 'or what.'" His voice was suddenly cold and his diction precise. "You will take me to the book, and you will do it now."

Maura twisted her torso and drove the knuckles of her free hand into Mansoor's solar plexus. Air whooshed out of him and he gasped for breath but would not let go. She drove the heel of her palm into his nose and felt it give with a satisfying crunch. This time, he let go and slumped backward, sitting hard on the gravel.

Maura yanked the van door open and scooped the keys from under the mat. She started the engine and pulled the shifter into reverse. Mansoor's hands hooked like claws, reached through the open window as she cracked the gas and the van hooked out into the street knocking him to the ground again. As she drove away, she could see him in her rearview mirror, staggering down the street screaming unheard words at her like some silent movie villain. Maura didn't need subtitles to know that she had just been cursed, and not with a simple hell or damn.

Mister Smith sat in the Cadillac up the alley from the glass shop. He saw Mansoor from behind, ranting and waving his arms like a lunatic.

Curses.

Spells.

Competition.

He looked around. Nobody in sight. Mister Smith pulled away from the curb and stepped on the gas. The big V-8 pushed the car to almost fifty by the time he hit Mansoor, whose body thumped under the wheels, front and rear. The Cadillac turned the corner and was gone, leaving Mansoor's broken body sprawled on the pavement.

"Now, darling," said Mister Smith, "Which way did you go?" He circled the soldier and headed west out of town, whistling "I'll Take you Home again, Kathleen."

LIX

"Singer knows what the book says, right? Why don't you let him use the gadget?" Swede leaned forward over the table. "Can you really trust the chick?"

"She knows a lot more about it than we do. She has some experience with magic. Singer doesn't. If he thinks for one second that she's doing anything to hurt us, he'll take her out."

"Yeah, but how will he know?"

"You said it yourself. He decoded the book. He knows what it says. If she steps off the path, he'll stop her."

"I trust you, Johnny, and I trust your judgment, but I'm not sure about her."

"I am," said Slate, and thought, because she knows enough to respect magic without fearing it. Singer is still too shaky right now, but once he gets used to it, he can take over and we won't need Maura anymore. Then, some hard decisions will have to be made, but for the moment, the bet has paid off. Let it ride.

LX

The hierarchy of law enforcement in Chambliss, like so many small towns in rural America, started with a local constable. Ed Guidry was his name, and his areas of expertise included hauling drunks to the town lockup, writing an occasional speeding ticket when he could actually catch the offender in his tired old Mercury, and confiscating beer from the local teens (which he usually drank with his buddies). He called in the Georgia Patrol when anything serious happened. Guidry took one look at Robert Mansoor's body, threw up in the gutter, and called the Patrol.

Beaudry and Grover arrived an hour later to find what looked like half the town milling around the hit-and-run scene. Someone had covered the body with a spattered painter's tarp. Guidry, still looking a little green, sat in the front seat of his prowl car.

"Okay, Ed," said Grover. "What do you know about all this?"

"Nobody saw it happen, but Ross from the glass shop said he heard an argument and some shouting a minute or two before it happened."

"Let's go talk to Ross," Beaudry said. "Ed, get off your ass and see if you can't get this crowd out of here. We don't need all of them meandering around. Did you check the body for I.D.?"

Guidry shook his head.

"Tom, you check the body. I'll go talk to Mister Ross.

He found Arnold Ross in his shop. The shop had no windows except the big one in the front and was dark as a cave, ironic for a glazier. Ross sat at his worktable under a buzzing rack of fluorescent lights that made his white hair glow, a cigarette in one hand and a cup of coffee in the other.

"Mister Ross," said Beaudry, "I understand that you have some information about the accident out front."

Ross coughed a deep rattling noise and took a drink of his coffee. "I didn't see it."

"But you heard something?"

"Yeah, I heard two people arguing outside, a man and a woman. They were going at it pretty good, then I heard a motor start, tires squeal, and the man kept screaming after her, some kind of gibberish in a foreign language."

"And you didn't see who it was?"

"They weren't in front of the shop, so I didn't see them, and it only lasted a minute or so. But I figure it was that girl I fixed the window for."

"Tell me about her," said Beaudry.

"She was a pretty thing, tall, long dark hair pulled back. But she looked hard, tough. She brought in a van with a broken back window, a white Ford Econoline. She needed it fixed in a hurry; paid me extra."

"Her name?"

"Didn't ask. She handed me cash."

"Did you write her a receipt?"

"Just wrote 'repair' and the amount, like I always do."

"And she left, you heard the argument, you heard the engine start and drive away. Was it her van?"

"It ain't out there now, so I guess that was it."

"But you heard the man still shouting at her after she pulled away?"

"Yep. He was yelling pretty loud."

"But you didn't go outside?"

"I learned a long time ago to mind my own business. Man and a woman argue; I figure it's between them. But when I heard the guy get hit, I went out. That's when I found him lying in the alley."

"You didn't see the van?"

Ross shook his head.

"Or any other vehicle?"

"Nope."

"Thank you, Mister Ross," said Beaudry. "I expect we'll be back to talk with you again."

Ross nodded. "I'll be here."

Outside, Grover had spread the contents of the victim's pockets on the hood of the patrol car. Keys, wallet, cigarettes, a handful of change, and a Buck knife. "Driver's license says he's Robert Mansoor, address is a post office box in Durham, North Carolina. Some money, but not much else that's helpful."

Beaudry flipped the keys over the ring one at a time. "Pontiac. Hey, Ed." Guidry came over. "Look up and down the street for a block or so in every direction. See if you find a Pontiac this key will fit." Guidry took the key and hurried off, glad to be away from the accident scene.

"So what did Ross say?"

"He said Mansoor was outside arguing with a girl before this happened. Tall girl, dark hair."

"Penny Winters?"

"Could be. Ross fixed a window in a van for her, but he says Mansoor was still shouting at her when she drove away."

"Maybe she drove around the block and picked him off the second time around."

"Get on the radio and get Macon to run a check on our Miss Winters."

"No APB on the van?"

"There must be about a thousand white Ford vans in Georgia. But there's really no need. I think we know where she's headed. After all, didn't that fellow say his buddy took the *van* to Atlanta?"

"Bet you five bucks it's white."

"Let's go find out. If there's a dent in the grille, we can wrap this one up quick."

Two men in suits shouldered through the crowd of rubberneckers. The shorter one smiled affably and flipped open a cred wallet to show a badge and photo I.D. "I'm agent Katz, FBI, and this is agent Barnes." He read the names. "Trooper Beaudry."

"That's Corporal Beaudry."

Katz smiled again. "Sorry, *Corporal* Beaudry, and you are?"

"Corporal Grover."

Katz nodded. "Got it. You two are the investigating officers here?"

"Yes, sir. If you don't mind me asking, what's the FBI doing looking at a hit-and-run?"

"All part of an ongoing investigation we can't discuss at the moment. We'll need your cooperation."

I'll bet you do, thought Beaudry resenting the agent's presumption.

"You've identified the vic?"

"Name's Robert Mansoor. Address is Durham, North Carolina."

"Where do the bodies go around here?"

"Bob Kennison's the Deputy Coroner. His funeral home in Shryock's the likeliest destination."

"I assume we can trust him to follow standard procedures, right?"

Beaudry took off his sunglasses so that he could look Katz square in the eye. "I don't suppose he'll hang the body up from a tree limb and dress it like a deer."

Katz ignored the jibe. "We'll need his prints to run through the Bureau files immediately. Are those his personal effects?"

"All these things were in his pockets," said Beaudry, not "these were all the things in his pockets," a clever way to not mention the car keys.

Katz scooped the wallet, knife and change from the hood of the car and dropped them into the pocket of his jacket. "So, did anybody see this happen?"

"Nobody saw anything," Beaudry said.

"Well, we're staying at the Cozy Nook Motel. Do us a favor and drop off a copy of your report." Katz smiled for the third time. "You boys have a nice day. Oh, and don't discuss this with anyone. We don't want the investigation compromised. Loose lips and all that."

The agents turned and strode away, and not a minute too soon. From the corner of his eye, Beaudry saw Ed hustling down the sidewalk. "Lazy bastards. Let them do their own work. I heard once that a Sheriff has authority that overrides Federals. You ever hear that, Tom?"

Grover said, "I heard that a Sheriff can order them out of his county and they have to go."

"We need to have a talk with Orville. I don't know how all this hooks up yet, but I do know I don't want people getting away because of the Feds pulling rank."

Ed saw them and trotted over, excited, his earlier queasiness forgotten. He held out Mansoor's keys to Beaudry. "I found it. The car's parked over on Elm Street three blocks from here. It's green and all beat to shit"

"Good work, Ed. We'll take it from here. And remember, Ed, the less said about this the better 'til we have a handle on who the driver is."

"Don't worry, fellows." Ed winked. "Mum's the word."

"Okay, Tom," said Beaudry climbing into the patrol car. "Let's go take a look at the Pontiac."

"So," Barnes said, pulling the car into the Cozy Nook. "You think this Mansoor guy is connected to all this?"

"We'll have to run his name through the files and see what pops up. You saw the guy. Shaggy long hair, Levi's and sandals, a Stop the War T-shirt. He's a hippie from Central Casting. And he's no young kid. I'm guessing he's in the drug trade. Look, Hannisford's Jeep isn't here. What a surprise."

"I'll be surprised when we find it if it doesn't have a man-sized dent in the bumper."

LXII

If Mansoor's Pontiac had ever been washed, it was by a rainstorm.

"Four new tires," said Grover. "Wonder why he'd waste that kind of money on a junker like this."

"Who knows?" Beaudry unlocked the driver door. The smell of days-old fast food refuse wafted out. "Smells like a god-damned garbage can." He leaned across the front seat and pulled the lock buttons up for the other doors.

The Pontiac looked like a mobile landfill. Trash, much of it food wrappers and soda cans filled the foot wells in the back almost to the edge of the seats. The passenger side in the front wasn't much better. The ashtray overflowed with butts and a half empty pack of Marlboros lay on the dashboard.

"Looks as if our boy's been spending a lot of time in his car lately." Grover poked in the backseat trash with his nightstick. "It's all garbage back here."

Beaudry slid under the steering wheel and felt a broken spring in the driver's seat. He reached across the dash and pushed the button on the glove compartment. A handful of papers fell out along with an amber plastic pharmacy bottle. In it were a half-dozen white tablets. "Look here, Tom." Beaudry shook the bottle gently so that he could see the facets of the pills. "No trade names or numbers."

"You think they're uppers?"

"I'm no expert, but I'd say offhand they aren't aspirins." Beaudry scooped out more papers from the glove box. "Car's registered to Robert Mansoor, same address as the driver's license."

Nothing more of note was found in the passenger compartment. Beaudry threw Grover they keys. "Check the trunk."

Grover turned the key in the lock. The trunk lid flew up and a huge dappled mastiff boiled out of it, jaws snapping.

"Jesus Christ!" Grover pulled his revolver from the holster but before he could get a shot off, the dog instinctively clamped its jaws on his gun hand. Grover's pistol clattered on the pavement.

His view blocked by the trunk lid, Beaudry couldn't see what was going on but in seconds, he was out of the car, gun in hand, in time to see the dog running down the street. Grover held his right hand in his left, blood dripping from the bite. "God-damned dog about took my hand off. Who keeps a dog in the trunk of his car?"

"Another question: why didn't the dog bark?"

Beaudry went back to the patrol car and got peroxide and a roll of gauze from the First Aid kit in the trunk. He swabbed the bites and wrapped Grover's hand. Before he was done, blood was already staining the white gauze crimson. "That's a bad bite, Tom. We've got to get you a tetanus shot."

"We aren't going after the dog?"

"Dog's long gone. I'll call Animal Control. I just hope they find it to make sure it isn't rabid. Otherwise, you'll have to have shots."

"Oh, hell, you're right. I had them one time before when I was a kid. Three days in a row through my gut. Hurt like a mother. I hope I don't have to go through that again. But before we do anything, let's see what was in that trunk that was so important he had the Hound of the Baskervilles guarding it."

The trunk was a disappointment to both of them. Besides a bald spare tire and a jack, they found a box of old books, a quilted mover's blanket, a water dish for the mastiff, and a duffel bag with some of Mansoor's clothes. "Nothing more to see here," Beaudry said slamming the trunk. Let's go get you that tetanus shot."

"Aren't we going out to the Parker place?"

"Hospital's on the way. Can you shoot left-handed or do I have to call for backup?"

...a huge dappled mastiff boiled out...

LXIII

Maura and Slate returned to the clearing where they'd parked the van and she thought at first the team had left without them. But as she got closer, she saw Singer building a small fire. Haines and Swede were sitting on a fallen tree drinking beer as if they were on a picnic. Looking more closely, she saw a tiny glint of chrome through camouflage netting and fresh cut brush.

"Wow. That's amazing. I know it's there and I still can hardly see it."

"Abracadabra," said Swede, wiggling his fingers. "We're the pros from Dover."

Slate set down his pack. "We found an area about two klicks from here that should do for tonight. If we leave right after moonset, we should make Pennsylvania before dark."

"What's in Pennsylvania?"

"Our backup camp. It's not as handy as the Parker place, but we can hole up there while we plan what comes next."

"And what comes next?"

"The third leg of the triangle: survival, escape, payback."

Maura looked at the ground and didn't say anything.

"That bother you?" said Slate.

"A little, but I understand you aren't going after a pack of Cub Scouts. You're doing what needs done."

"It's what we do." He turned to Singer. "What's for supper?"

"Thursday's Thanksgiving, and since we don't know where we'll be, I figured we'd celebrate early. How's turkey, dressing, and sweet potatoes sound—with cranberry sauce, of course."

"Where would you get a turkey?" Maura said.

"Uncle Sam." Singer threw a metal tin about twice the size of a sardine can to her. The top panel read: MRE Turkey Dinner.

She shook her head. "Unbelievable."

Swede shrugged. "Like I said, 'abracadabra.'"

LXIV

The sky darkened with clouds as Beaudry and Grover walked up the lane to the camp. They opted to leave their cruiser at the turn-off and approach on foot rather than allow the sound of the car to give them away.

Grover's empty holster flap was closed and his pistol rode at the small of his back in his waistband within reach of his left hand. His right was rebandaged even more restrictively by the emergency room doctor who advised him to not use it for a few days. "Hand's starting to throb," he said, grimacing.

"Shoulda taken the morphine."

"Can't shoot straight on dope."

"That's a good point."

They came near the bend in the lane and stepped off the wheel tracks into the brush. In a moment they could see the antenna projecting from the cabin, then the cabin, then the camp.

"Damn. The van's not here." Beaudry hissed.

"Nothing's moving. Looks like the vets aren't here either. Told you we should've come here first, not go to the hospital."

"Maybe there's somebody inside. Let's check it out." They broke cover and moved cautiously to the back of the cabin. Beaudry unsnapped his holster and kept his hand on the butt of his pistol.

No sound from inside. They waited until the birds started chirping again. "Nobody around the outside," Grover said.

Beaudry gave a twitch of his head. "I'll go around this way, and you go that way and watch the porch from the corner. Look sharp. These boys are tricky." They split up and each went his way around the cabin.

Beaudry reached the porch steps and called out. "Georgia Patrol." No response.

He drew his pistol and gave Grover a motion to follow him but keep his distance. He took the steps one at a time, every nerve on high alert. "Georgia Patrol," he called out again.

The porch looked the same as his last visit. A few beer cans and a makeshift ashtray that looked like a sardine can full of gray ash sat on the table. No butts, Beaudry thought. They field strip their cigarettes. The door was open behind the screen but the cabin was dark inside.

He knocked on the screen door and it rattled in its frame. "Hello, inside. Georgia Patrol. I'm coming in." He pulled the door open and the hinges groaned. Grover was on the porch by now, his revolver aimed at the dark doorway. Beaudry stepped inside.

His eyes adjusted quickly to the dim room and he knew immediately that the cabin was empty. Plates on the table, pots in the sink. A skillet with congealing fry grease sat on the stove. They weren't gone long.

He saw two deer rifles, a .410 shotgun and a single shot .22 varmint gun in a rack on the wall behind the door. Boxes of shells sat below on a crude shelf, pairs of muddy boots stood in a row on the floor. Jackets and hats hung from nails driven in the plank walls.

Beaudry opened a cupboard over the sink. It was full of foodstuffs. Two cases of beer sat on the floor beside the sink.

In the bedroom they found four cots and duffel bags packed mostly with clothing and personal effects; razors, toothbrushes, a hairbrush. The place looked for all the world as if they had left it for an hour and would be back any minute. Then it hit him. On a table at the back of the bedroom was a Citizen's Band radio, but there was no shortwave unit. They'd taken it with them.

He stepped back onto the porch and saw Grover coming from the dock. "Air boat's gone."

"The motorcycle?"

"It's gone too."

Beaudry chewed his lower lip. "Let's get back to the car and put out the APB on the van and the airboat. Everything in that cabin's set to look as if they'll be back any time now, but they took the short wave. They're running. To make it worse, it looks as if they've split up maybe three different ways."

"What about the Feds?"

"Cat's out of the sack," Beaudry shook his head in disgust and stared out across the lake. "To catch this bunch we're gonna need all the help we can get. I want to get the lab boys down here to dust everything in the place for prints."

They were halfway down the lane to their cruiser when the cabin went up in a roar and a ball of flame. Grover and Beaudry stared at the plume of smoke rising over the trees. If there had been any evidence in the cabin, it was gone forever.

Grover whistled. "Like you said about needing help."

LXV

Katz and Barnes were waiting at the Kozy Nook when Hannisford and Poston came back from setting the cameras. Their car was parked out of sight away from the building. "Here they come," said Barnes, nudging Katz awake. "And it doesn't look like the Jeep hit a damned thing."

"Crap. I was hoping. I hate to let these birds walk away, but we don't have anything substantial to hold them on."

The pair had gotten a call from the field office to shut down the operation in Chambliss. Bank robbers cut a swath through northern Florida and into Georgia the past three days. As soon as the crooks went interstate, it became an FBI case, and all available personnel were reassigned to hunt down what the newspapers were calling "a modern-day Bonnie and Clyde."

"Do I tell them or do you?" said Katz.

"You do it," said Barnes. "You're Mister Personality."

They approached the Jeep as Poston and Hannisford were climbing out. "Good news for you boys," said Katz. "You're free to go."

"Just like that? What happened?"

Barnes shot Hannisford a hard look. "Don't ask questions, idiot. Just smile and say 'thank you' before we change our minds."

"I still think you two are dirty," said Katz, "and you're still on the radar, but my advice is for you to leave Chambliss and don't come back." The agents walked to their car, got in, and drove away leaving Hannisford and Poston standing in the parking lot.

"That was a lucky break," said Poston. "Grab your stuff from the room and let's get out of here."

"What about the cameras in the swamp? I'm not leaving all that equipment. Besides, Elroy, don't you want to see if we catch your werewolf?"

"There are other motels in the towns around here. We'll hole up in one of them for a day or two."

In ten minutes, they were on the road.

LXVI

The site Slate and Maura chose for the first turning of the full moon was a clearing at the edge of the lake about a mile from the van. Trees and brush ringed it on three sides and a bank hung over the water at the fourth. Slate opened the box and handed the amulet still wrapped in the blue cloth to Maura.

"I thought I wasn't going to try to use the *farkas ostor* until tomorrow night."

"Contingencies," Slate said. "Between the cops and Mansoor, we don't have the luxury of hanging around here for three nights. We're going to have to travel during the change cycle, and if the amulet will help, so much the better."

"I understand how it works and what words to say, but I can't guarantee anything."

"If it doesn't work now, there's more we can learn."

"Yes, there's always more."

She walked ahead and Slate hung back to talk to Singer. "You know what to do."

"Sure, stop her if she does anything out of line, but how will I know?"

"She may not know herself. It's all a crapshoot. Trust your gut. If it feels wrong, stop her anyway you have to. We've survived without the amulet up to now, and if it doesn't work, this time, we can always try again later."

"I don't like it, Johnny."

"Me either, but we have to take the chance."

The last gray of twilight was full of rumbling thunder and distant flashes of lightning. A rainstorm was on the way. When they reached the clearing, the team disrobed and squatted naked on the thick grass. The swamp was silent for a moment as the livestock took the measure of the newcomers, then gradually came back to life with the call of the night birds, the chittering of cicadas and the occasional grunt and splash of an alligator.

As they waited, Maura ran the incantations through her mind, afraid to say them aloud too soon.

Singer came up behind her. "You okay?"

"It's just a lot all at once. Waiting is the worst part."

Singer lit two cigarettes and handed one to her. She took a drag from it and let the smoke out in a long white stream.

"How long, Singer?" Haines said.

"Two minutes to show time."

The horizon was lightening. The edge of the moon would creep over it soon.

Maura ground the cigarette under her boot. She unwrapped the amulet and found the violet gemstone in the center was already faintly glowing. She stepped a few paces back, putting distance between herself and the naked men. She held her breath.

Moonrise.

The turn began and Maura stared rapt at the convulsive changes. Her jaw sagged at the sight of men becoming monsters, faces bristling with dark tufts of hair, jaws elongating into fanged snouts, limbs and joints distending, and human eyes glowing a feral yellow. Nothing she had learned in years of research and study prepared her for what she saw.

On one hand, a natural revulsion tugged at her, instinctively screaming at her to cover her eyes, to flee, while at the same time, her curiosity rooted her to the spot, desperate to know what came next.

"Maura, use the amulet."

She was so stunned by the transformation that she had forgotten for a moment what she was doing there. She began the incantation and as she spoke the words, the *farkas ostor* blazed, radiating violet light that bathed the clearing to the trees at its edge in a purple glow. She held it high in her outstretched hand.

The men stopped writhing in pain; they stopped moaning; they lay still on the ground as the change ran its course. One by one they stood, no longer human, now furred horrors that could kill with a blow, disembowel with a swipe of their wicked claws. Maura felt the thrill of discovery, but she felt no fear. Instead, she felt joined to them.

Something simple. "Join hands." She said it in French and immediately wondered if she should have said it in English, but the werewolves placed their paws one over the other. Maura felt a thrill she'd never felt before. Werewolves. Real werewolves and they were obeying her command. "Hands high." They raised their arms over their heads.

She felt a tug at her brain and her concentration faltered. The pack dropped its paws. What was wrong?

A powerful arm whipped around her throat and the *farkas ostor* was snatched from her hand.

"I'll take that little bauble, lass." The violet glow made Mister Smith's face with its gap-toothed leer a hellish mask.

Slate and the team rushed snarling at Smith, who calmly raised the amulet and spoke in a strange language. The werewolves froze in midstride and the charge became a bizarre diorama.

"Let her go." Singer pointed his automatic over Maura's shoulder at Mister Smith's grinning head. "And drop the amulet." He cocked the hammer. "Now."

Singer felt something slithering through the convolutions of his brain. He saw the team rush at him, claws slashing, fangs bared then snapped back to reality.

"Don't be foolish, boy," said Smith. "A word from me and your furry friends will have you and the girl for supper. And you do fear them so."

Cold sweat popped out on Singer's forehead. His gun hand trembled.

"Shoot him," Slate snarled, but Singer dropped his pistol.

"Good lad." Smith dragged Maura back a few steps. "You all just stay as you are. Now, my sweet, tell me, where did you learn to use this pretty trinket?"

Maura's mouth opened and closed but nothing came out.

"You will tell me." Smith's grip tightened on her throat.

At that moment, a hundred eighty pounds of red-eyed dappled fury leapt from the darkness. Janus, Mansoor's mastiff clamped its bear trap jaws on Mister Smith's wrist. The *farkas ostor* went spinning through the air. The werewolves were still immobile, waiting for a command.

Maura sank to her knees gasping for air and suddenly realized what she had to do. She scrambled on all fours for the purple glow in the tall grass.

Mister Smith wrestled with the dog, hands around its neck, barely able to hold it away as it snapped at his throat.

Maura found the *farkas ostor* and held it high. What to say? What did Smith tell them?

Singer scooped up his gun but before he could fire it, man and dog fell backward over the bank into the lake and sank out of sight. They broke the surface quickly, thrashing in mortal combat.

Singer strained his eyes. He couldn't see for a shot. Then he heard other splashes. The gators were joining the party.

"Move!" Maura shouted and the team suddenly broke from their poses, dazed from the magic Smith had worked on them.

In the dark water. Singer heard more thrashing than a dog and a man could make. The werewolves ran toward the bank and Maura made a decision. She called out, "Stop!"

As one the pack halted, snarling, chests heaving, aching to dive into the water and rend the intruder to pieces.

Soon the thrashing stopped. The alligators were gone.

Singer stood at the edge of the bank staring at the dark water for five minutes. Not a ripple. "Who the hell was that guy?"

"No idea, but he knew how to use the *farkas ostor* better than I do." Maura made another decision. She held the amulet high and said to the team, "Back to the van."

The werewolves turned and loped noiselessly through the brush the way they had come.

Singer said, "What are you doing?"

"We know this works now," she said, staring at the glowing amulet in her palm. "It's safe to travel with them as they are. We have to get away from here right now before somebody else like him..." she shuddered, "... shows up. Can you get us out of here fast?"

Singer nodded. "I've got a half-dozen escape routes all on back roads and logging trails that'll take us out of the state in two hours."

"Then let's go. We don't dare wait for morning."

At the van, the team was waiting. Maura and Singer pulled away the camouflage and Maura opened the rear doors. "Inside." The team climbed in. "Sit." They did.

Maura took her place with them, sitting in a lotus position and cradling the amulet in her palm. "Sleep." Heads dropped to furred chests and the werewolves were still.

"Okay, Singer, get us out of here."

LXVII

Beaudry steered the commandeered Zodiac as Grover swept the surface of the swamp with a spotlight. Rain pelted the swamp as hard as a hailstorm. Beaudry figured the roadblocks would take care of the van, and he concentrated on the air boat. Two other teams were combing other parts of the area, but so far none of them had found a trace of the fugitives.

"Hey, Alan, slow down," Grover said. "Look over there."

Beaudry cut the Zodiac's motor and strained his eyes. In a small inlet half hidden by cypress roots and Spanish moss, he could see the glint of a spidery metal frame. He pulled the boat into the inlet. They recognized the pancake cage of the sunken airboat.

"Son of a bitch," said Grover. "Well, now we know they aren't on the water. Now, what?"

"Now we double up on the roadblocks. I'm betting they're all in that white van."

LXVIII

The winch on the front of the van whined as it pulled the fallen tree from the road if you could call it that, little more than a pair of overgrown ruts with brush and branches that dragged the sides of the van as it crawled through the darkness. The winch had come in handy once earlier that night when the van became mired in a mud hole courtesy of the steady hammering downpour.

Singer studied a map in the green glow of the dashboard lights. Beside him, a police band radio crackled and stuttered with messages from the Georgia Patrol. "From what I can see by the map, we're past the roadblocks on the main highways now. They threw the net too close, but we'll stay on the back roads 'til we're out of Georgia. The APB is statewide and we can't risk being stopped."

"Well, let me know as soon as we hit the state line. I can't wait to come up for air." The oily animal funk of the werewolves in the closed van had quickly given Maura a headache. Her adrenaline rush had worn off and deep fatigue set in. When this was over, she'd sleep for a week.

LXIX

MacDonald hung up the phone. The chatter on the police radio from Georgia had made its way to Langley and he was yanked out of a sound sleep to come to headquarters. The Georgia Patrol officer, a guy named Beaudry told him a story about four men and a woman holed up in a compound in Georgia. MacDonald faxed the pictures of Slate and his crew to Macon, and Beaudry confirmed their I.D.s.

Damn. MacDonald slammed his fist on the desk. They're here and they're all together. He couldn't blame Beaudry and the Georgia Patrol for letting them escape. Slate and his team weren't just professionals; they were the best at what they did.

And what was the FBI doing in Chambliss, Georgia? Beaudry was vague on that score but probably wasn't told much anyway. Mac couldn't just drop in at the Bureau and ask. The Company technically wasn't allowed to operate domestically, and if people looked too close, they'd tumble to the black bag operation in Laos and the cover up that started this whole mess.

He picked up the phone again and dialed Briggs's number. He'd catch a lot of flak from Briggs, but waking him at this ungodly hour made it almost worthwhile.

Briggs was awake. "Good news, I hope," he said.

"Not much. We have confirmation that Slate and his team are alive and in country. They were hiding out in Georgia and slipped away from the locals. They're at large."

Mac listened to Briggs breathe for a while. "Find them."

"What I'm afraid of is they're going to find you. And they already know where to look."

"How would they know?"

"Parker, if he wasn't double-crossing the man in the parking garage. He was around when the Laos operation went tits up. And he wasn't exactly your best friend."

Briggs thought it over. "They'll figure by now that we know they're all stateside. If they make a move on me, it'll be soon before we get another fix on them. Call the Dream Team."

"They're in the field."

"Bring them back. If Slate and his men come after me, they'll find a hard target." Briggs hung up.

MacDonald stared at the mute receiver in his hand. The Dream Team. The Company's elite assassination squad. Four of the coldest, most efficient killers on earth. Put them in the same room with Slate's team and see who walks out.

What was the old Chinese curse? He said it aloud: "May you live in interesting times."

LXX

Billy and Jake were waiting on the steps of the First National Bank of Chambliss when the doors opened. Jake had the check in his hand; they'd both signed the back. Jake handed it to the teller. "Can we have it in tens and twenties?"

The dowdy teller, whose nameplate beside her cage read Dorothy, said, "I'll need to see identification from both of you."

"Yeah, sure." Jake reached for his wallet. He pulled out his driver's license and Billy did the same. Dorothy studied the licenses, comparing their names to the endorsement signatures. She turned the check over and stamped it with red ink.

"Do you have an account here?"

"No, but my dad does," said Billy.

"Because this check is written on an out of state bank, we can't cash it for you until it clears."

"Well, how long will that take?"

"Normally, two days."

Billy turned to Jake. "Do you think we could cash it someplace else? Maybe at the hardware store or the supermarket?"

"I don't know whether they would take it now," Dorothy said. "It's already been stamped received by First National."

"Oh, man, we didn't know. Isn't there any way you could help us out?"

Dorothy shook her head. "Sorry, boys; it's bank policy." She pointed to a sign on the wall listing the bank's rules for account holders and others.

She wrote a receipt, stamped it with another of the dozen rubber stamps that hung from a chromed swivel tree beside her. "It should be clear by Wednesday, but you can check back tomorrow."

Jake and Billy stared at the receipt. "We'll be back tomorrow." As they left, Jake muttered under his breath, "Bitch."

"Now what?" Billy said.

"Now we head for school and try to sneak into second-period gym class without getting caught."

LXXI

The backup camp was tucked in a hollow three miles from the last paved road if you thought of tarred gravel as pavement. The ride was long and uncomfortable, but it was over.

At moonset, the team turned without incident, still asleep from Maura's command. One by one they woke.

"Well, I guess it worked," said Swede, pulling on his jeans. "Didn't hurt like before."

"No, it didn't," Haines agreed.

Slate was silent. He was studying Maura closely. She finally met his eyes. "What?"

"Why did you call us off? We should have killed the guy in the swamp."

"Because the alligators were doing the job for you," she said, "and you'd have been playing in their backyard. What if one of them pulled you under? You're a werewolf, not Superman. How long can a werewolf hold its breath? Have you tried it?"

"She's got you there, Johnny," said Swede. "Don't mind him, honey, Johnny never was good at taking orders."

Slate didn't say anything else, but Maura knew they'd have the discussion again.

The camp was a cluster of tar paper shacks that looked as if a good wind would blow them over. A stovepipe stuck out of the roof of the largest one. The rusted shell of a pickup truck sat on its axles with a small tree growing up through the open hood. "It ain't the Hilton," quipped Haines, "but it's home."

Maura climbed out of the van stretching her back and legs. The ride was punishing and she was looking forward to some sleep before the next moonrise.

"Don't wander off," Slate said. "We have to disable the perimeter security before you go strolling in the woods."

"Security?"

"Booby traps," said Haines. "Discourages the locals."

Singer came out of the largest shack. "Pretty much picked clean."

Slate shrugged. "Did you expect anything different?"

Swede was dragging a heavy tow chain from the back of the van. "Time to open the vault."

"What vault?"

"If we left things in plain sight, the good old boys up here would cart it all away before we were five miles down the road, and if we just dug a hole in the woods, they'd find it sooner or later, so we left a token set of gear behind where they could find it and hid what we'd need later."

Swede hooked one end of the tow chain to the frame of the pickup and the other to the winch mounted on the front of the van. "Let's see how it goes."

He hopped into the driver's seat of the van and started the engine. The winch whined the cable strained, and the derelict pickup began to swing away from its resting place, the tree through its engine compartment acting as a pivot. An opossum darted from its nest underneath the hulk. Branches snapped and the truck's frame groaned as it turned ninety degrees from its original position.

Maura looked at the exposed ground. "I still don't see anything."

"That's because we're good at what we do. It's undisturbed." Haines walked around the side of the van with two shovels. He threw one to Swede. "Let's start digging."

What lay six feet beneath the surface was a coffin. Symbols were painted on its lid, some of which Maura recognized as Hex Signs from Amish country and others she'd found in her studies of Appalachian folklore.

"The hillbillies up here are a superstitious lot. If they figured out something was buried under the truck and dug down, they'd see those markings and run like the Devil was after them." Haines got behind the coffin and heaved up one end. "Give me a hand, Swede, and let's get this bastard out of the ground."

The lock was rusted and stubborn, so Swede pried the lid open with a tire iron. Inside it was packed solid with an array of weapons. Maura recognized some of the firearms from news photos she'd seen of Viet Nam.

Others looked like older ordnance from World War II. Tucked around the guns and ammo were MREs, a medical kit, and other supplies.

"Where did you get all this stuff?"

"Midnight shopping at the National Guard Armory in Cumberland." Swede hefted a grenade in his palm. "Your tax dollars at work."

LXXII

Billy and Jake went back to First National just before closing time. There was a line at Dorothy's window, the only one open. Billy never understood why a bank would have six windows and keep most of them closed. He craned his neck to count the people ahead of him and saw Roxy at Dorothy's window. She turned away from the teller's cage with a smile on her face. When she saw Billy and Jake, her smile faded then returned as she pulled a wad of money from the pocket of her jeans. She fanned a bunch of twenties, bobbed her head, folded the money and put it back into her pocket. As he watched her walk away, Billy felt sick.

When they got to the window, Jake said, "Was there any news on our check?"

"Yes, we got word on it a little while ago." Dorothy dug through some papers and pulled out the check from *Unidentified*. She slid it under the grille to them. Jake turned it over and saw another rubber stamp on it: Stopped Payment.

"What's that mean?" he asked Dorothy, who shrugged and said. "It means the check won't clear because the source cancelled payment. We can't cash it. You'll have to take it up with the people who wrote the check." She looked over his shoulder at the customer behind them and said, "Next."

LXXIII

Hannisford hung the blankets from the double bed over the bathroom window to create a makeshift darkroom in the Morgan's Inn Motel in

Rockland. It wasn't the greatest, but it would do. Poston had retrieved the cameras a few hours before and three of them had been tripped. The cameras were set where high-grade film and a slow shutter speed coupled with the light from a full moon would give a reasonable photo.

Film from the first two caught a deer and a wild pig, respectively. The third was something else altogether. "Hey, Elroy," he said, pulling the eight-by-ten from the tray. "You gotta see this."

"What is it?" Poston said, excitement rising in his voice.

"I'm not exactly sure."

Hannisford laid the wet print on the scarred motel dresser and dragged the lamp closer to shine its dim light on the picture.

The man was tall but hunchbacked, his crooked teeth bared in a grimace of pain. He was wearing a dark suit that clung to him like wet rags and cradling an injured arm.

"Who the hell is that?" said Hannisford.

"And what's he doing in the swamp wearing a suit?"

LXXIV

Grover stuck his head into the day room. "Ran the plate on the Caddy."

Beaudry looked up from the typewriter where he'd been two-finger pecking a report on the hit-and-run. "And?"

"It's registered to a fake name at a fake address in Newark, New Jersey."

"We'll know soon from the lab whether the blood on the car matches Mansoor's type."

"I'm betting it does, considering we found it in a Mansoor-shaped dent in the grille."

"Any word back from the Federales?"

"Nope. I've called the field office in Atlanta three times. Katz and Barnes aren't in and they aren't calling back."

"Next time you call, Tom, leave a message that we found the car that hit Mansoor. Maybe they'll call back then. I'm more curious than anything to see who owns those prints we lifted from the steering wheel."

"I'll be glad when this is over. My family thinks I ran away and joined a carnival. Do you think we'll ever know exactly what was going on?"

Beaudry tipped his chair back, leaned his head against the wall and closed his eyes. "Based on my experience dealing with the FBI, probably not."

LXXV

Briggs called MacDonald into his office. "Any word from Georgia?"

"Nothing new; of course, you really didn't expect anything did you? I mean, this is Slate we're talking about. They're gone; they've covered their tracks, end of story."

Briggs gave him a cold stare. "I'm in danger as long as that bunch is running free. And if I'm in danger, so are you. Got it?"

Mac returned the stare. "Yeah, I got it. Where's the Dream Team?"

"They'll arrive at 1400 hours local time."

Mac questioned the need for the whole team to protect one pencil-pusher, but Briggs called the shots. If it were me and not him, thought Mac, I'd be twisting in the wind.

"How long do we have them?"

"Until Slate and his men are dead. The Committee gave me *carte blanche*."

Of course, thought Mac, because the Dream Team's protecting that bunch of jackals too. "So what do you want me to do?"

"What else? Keep looking for Slate until you find him. It's not just my ass now, Mac; it's yours."

LXXVI

"Do you think it's safe to use the *farkas ostor* again?" Singer said.

Maura sat, knees to her chin beside Slate and Singer looking over a long drop into a river gorge that cut between two of the mountains. Her breath plumed in the frosty air. "Robert called it an 'unshielded spell.' That's how he found me; he and that other creep."

Slate stared across the valley at the wall of pines on the other side as if looking for the answer to her question. "Mansoor found you before we turned. He must have picked up on the amulet when you tried it out the day before. That must be how our friend from last night happened to be in the neighborhood."

"Makes sense," said Maura. "Do you have any idea who he is?"

"Judging by how he handled the *farkas ostor*, I'd say he's a wizard like Pegg."

"Do you think he's that man Greystone that Robert was talking about?"

Slate shook his head. "I got the impression from what Mansoor told us that Greystone stays in the shadows and lets other people do his dirty work."

"Like the Company," Singer said.

"Like the Company. I'm guessing our man last night was somebody's agent, maybe Greystone's maybe somebody else's."

"Minion," Maura said. "They call them minions."

"Adds up to the same thing. And didn't Mansoor say there were others like Greystone around? We can't use the amulet if it's going to act like a beacon every time."

Singer said, "These people may be wizards, but they have to travel, right?"

"What's your point?"

"Think about it, Johnny. If we don't use the magic twice in the same place, if we move around, they can't get a fix on us."

"Not tonight. Tonight we turn without it. We'll save it for Fairfax."

"In the meantime," Maura said, "there is something else we can do."

Singer looked over to her. "Translate more of the book."

"Yes, and learn how to mask the spell."

Slate looked once again across the gorge. "I was afraid you'd say that." He turned to Maura. "What was it you told me? 'In for a penny, in for a buck.' I just don't want to dig a hole so deep we can't climb out of it."

LXXVII

The Dream Team arrived on schedule. The assassins were known to Mac only as letters of the Geek alphabet, Gamma, Delta, Theta, and Kappa.

"Do you have any idea who he is?"

When one of the team died, his letter was retired and the new man got the next available one. Mac wondered more than once what would happen when they got to Omega.

They sat like waxworks in the briefing room, four variations on the same character with the same haircut and the same suit. None of them smoked, none of them coughed, none of them blinked, it seemed, as MacDonald laid out the situation. Eight eyes fixed on him like a target. "And that's it," Mac said, finishing the briefing. The silence that followed was palpable. No one moved. Mac began to sweat, cold rivulets that ran between his shoulders to the crack of his ass.

Finally, Theta spoke. "You're certain it's Slate."

"As certain as we can be," said Mac.

Theta smiled.

LXXVIII

Moonrise.

Without the *farkas ostor* the change was as violent as ever. Maura stared as the team became the other, fascinated at the transformation, but horrified at the racking pain the change entailed. Once finished, however, the team rose to its feet, ready to run. At a signal from Slate, they disappeared into the moon shadows of the forest.

Maura shivered, as much from the mountain cold as from what she'd witnessed. She picked up the notebook that slipped unnoticed from her fingers. She recorded the time and details of the change. The more she knew about the phenomenon, she reasoned, the more she could help.

Maura didn't follow the pack. She could never keep up their pace. But she wanted more than anything to pursue them, to watch them in action, like observing animals in their natural habitat, but for the team, no habitat was natural, and they were not animals nor were they men; they were monsters by the strictest definition.

"Now what do we do?" she said to Singer.

"We wait."

They crouched beside the camp's fire pit taking turns feeding wood as the fire burned down, like primitive tribesmen warily keeping the darkness and the terrors it harbored at bay.

"What else is in the book?"

Maura stared over the flames into the trees. "The keys to power, the secrets of the universe, the wisdom of the ages. Take your pick. Whatever it is, people who know kept it out of reach for a long time."

"But you can't stop discovery, right? Look at the atom bomb. If we went back in time and killed Oppenheimer and all the scientists in the Manhattan Project, somebody else would have put it together eventually. Same thing with the book. Keeping it locked up won't keep its secrets forever."

"But it buys us time, a little more innocence, a little more Lamb before the Tyger comes along. I'm not sure I'd want to live in a world the grimoire could create."

"And today's that much better?"

"Better the evil we know."

LXXIX

Slate sat on his haunches on a flat span of limestone staring into the rapids. Whitewater swirled around the rocks in the river and the full moon sparkled on the ripples. Maura's question posed a curiosity and a challenge. He signaled the team to wait. Slate took a deep breath and dove headlong into the river.

The icy water jolted him like electricity. His instincts told him to claw for the surface, but he fought them back and kicked his way deeper among the submerged rocks. Fighting buoyancy he dribbled air from the corners of his mouth and clung to a rocky projection near the pebbled river bottom.

The shock worn off, the frigid water began numbing him now. How long had he been under? It seemed little more than a minute. Slate felt his lungs burning and he had to fight the urge of his diaphragm to buck and breathe in water that would surely drown him. He felt blackness squeeze around him like a deadly crushing hand and just as consciousness was slipping away, he let go of the rock.

Slate broke the surface and gasped in a breath. Then another. Haines and Swede were waiting where he'd left them. Haines gave a thumbs up. Slate returned the gesture and swam for shore. He climbed onto the rock and shook off water like a wet dog in from a thunderstorm.

How long can a werewolf hold its breath? No longer than a man.

The bottom edge of the moon was touching the tops of the trees. Slate turned his finger in the air and snarled. "Camp." Swede led and Slate brought up the rear. The cold didn't bother the others at all, their breath making ghostly puffs of steam. The run warmed Slate quickly and soon the icy plunge in the river was all but forgotten.

He smelled the camp before he saw it. Wood smoke, gun grease, and the woman. Was she safe with them? They were well disciplined as men and didn't mix survival with pleasure, but if the beast takes over, they might find out too late.

"They're back." Singer stood. He looked at his watch. "Moonset should be any time now."

Maura looked beyond the fire and saw three pairs of eyes glowing through the trees. The team strode into the clearing, pelts gleaming in the firelight. They stayed back from the fire pit. as wolves would do, and sat on their hands and haunches, facing Maura and Singer across the flames.

Singer gave a thumbs up and Slate returned the gesture. Maura had no trouble telling them apart. Swede, because of his size, was obvious. Haines's height and lanky build made him easy to tag. What distinguished Slate most was the air of self-possession he emanated, a sense of control the other two hadn't quite cultivated. His golden eyes stared back at her and she involuntarily shuddered in spite of herself.

Moonset.

The return to human was a world apart from last night's gentle transformation. Maura had preempted much of the trauma with the amulet the last time, but tonight she saw the change in all of its gore and agony. It left the men lying on the ground, bathed in sweat and shivering in front of the fire.

Swede was the first to stand up. He shook his head to clear it. "I gotta say, guys, I like it a lot better with the gadget."

● ● ●

The morning was gray and cold, the grass white with frost. Maura was crouched by the fire stirring a pot of oatmeal when Slate came out of the shack. "We need to talk."

"Okay, just you and I, not the others?"

"For the moment. You've studied werewolves; so have I, but I've also read a lot about wolf behavior. You?"

"Not as much."

"I'll get to the point. What happens if you're fertile on a full moon and we sense it? Do we try to mate with you? And do we fight each other for the privilege?"

Maura stared at Slate, then chuckled, then laughed out loud, great cathartic guffaws that echoed through the trees and unraveled all the anxiety and tension that built up over the past three days.

"What?" said Slate. "What's so funny?"

"Courting behavior. The thought of three werewolves lined up, one with a bouquet of roses, one with a heart shaped box of chocolates, and one with a bottle of champagne."

Then Slate laughed too.

"John, I don't think you have to worry on that score. I've been on the pill for years. I couldn't risk getting pregnant on a six-month trek into the jungle or the steppes. Romantic encounters aside, I could have been abducted by natives, raped by bandits—who knows what? There's no fertility to sense. Besides, if I'm using the *farkas ostor*, I think I can manage a horny werewolf."

Singer stepped out of the shack slapping his crossed arms over his chest. "What's so funny?"

Slate and Maura grinned at each other and Slate said, "You wouldn't believe me if I told you."

Singer warmed his hands over the fire. "So when do we leave for Fairfax?"

"It's two hundred miles, give or take. Maybe an hour."

"I'll go shake the boys awake."

LXXX

MacDonald came into the kitchen of Briggs's house to find Theta eating a plate of bacon and eggs right beside Kappa who had spread his disassembled Walther PPK over the kitchen table and was cleaning it with a rag and gun oil. The seven rounds were lined up like soldiers in formation, their brass gleaming, wiped clean of fingerprints. Both men looked up at Mac, stared at him for a three-count and went back to what they were doing. Gamma was covering the back of Briggs's two-acre property with a Mauser sniper rifle from an open upstairs window and Delta was concealed out front in the shrubbery.

None of them had said or done anything to indicate dislike, contempt, or condescension toward Mac, but they didn't have to. In fact, they paid no more attention to him, a trained and experienced field agent than they would a fly, affording him no more difficulty or consideration to eliminate should he get in their way.

Mac wasn't sure why Briggs kept him there. He could have run the search for Slate and his team more efficiently from headquarters. Maybe Briggs wanted him close to keep a hand on the operation.

A sudden idea gave him a chill. Maybe Briggs thought he was in league with Parker and he wanted him in reach in case he was right. Briggs was a sociopath, no doubt about it; that's why he ran the shop. But who knew what boiled under that Princeton haircut. And for that matter, who knew what Briggs knew that he wasn't telling Mac; otherwise, why the urgency for such heavy-duty protection. Paranoia, or informed self-interest? No matter, the result was the same.

Mac strolled into the den and looked out the window. The neighborhood, if you wanted to call it that, comprised a series of sprawling lots, most of them two acres along a paved lane, one way in and one way out. The houses were big, their grounds landscaped to give the look of a benign forest like you might find in a Disney cartoon. The grass was manicured, the shrubs were barbered, and the trees were limbed to give the look of wild but not wild. They call the place Hunterwood, thought Mac. I call it Plasticville, like the houses and buildings from the Lionel trains he played with as a kid.

Most of the people in this suburban paradise worked for the

Government and spent their days in D.C. stoking and oiling the machine that chewed people up like beef in a grinder then they spent their nights feet up in a lawn chair with a stiff drink deluding themselves that they were performing a noble service.

Men like Slate were sabots in the gears, and Mac and the Dream Team were there to see that the machine kept running, whatever the cost.

"Let them come." Mac turned from the window. Briggs stood in the doorway in tennis whites and a baby blue cable knit sweater with a tall fluted glass in his hand. "They won't leave alive." Briggs sipped his drink. "Mimosa," he said, "Champagne and orange juice. You should try one when you're not working."

"Why do I get the impression that you know more about this situation than you're telling me?"

Briggs gave Mac a thin smile. "Need to know, Mac. It's all need to know."

"If I'm supposed to protect you, how can I do it if I don't know all the details?"

"You know enough already." Briggs raised his glass and walked away, leaving Mac alone.

The thought landed on Mac like a deadfall: kill Slate and his team, and I'm the last loose end. Keep your friends close and your targets closer. He reached for the .32 automatic under his arm and dropped the clip. It was empty, probably cleaned out when he spent an hour fitfully dozing in a chair. He jacked the slide. They got the round in the chamber too.

I'll watch for my chance, Briggs, Mac thought, and if Slate doesn't kill you and your dogs don't kill me first, you and I are going to have a reckoning.

LXXXI

Mick Wallace would remember later that the man who came in that Tuesday was tall, short haired, needed a shave and never took off his aviator sunglasses, but few other details. The aerial photography business was slow like it always was in the winter season, and when the guy came in with a fifty dollar bill, Mick grabbed it up with no questions.

The tall man came in with a topographical map of the Fairfax area and asked for photos of a three square mile plot. Mick pulled them out of the files and he bought them on the spot. No problem; Mick had the negs and could print new copies any time.

"So, said Mick as he pocketed the fifty. "Are these part of some project?"

Mike Haines grinned. "Urban renewal."

The aerial photos told Slate what he needed to know. The rural Hunterwood Community where Briggs's house stood had only one road in, but an unpaved gas company service road ran within two hundred yards of the back of the house. From there they could move through the trees and come up behind the place with minimum exposure after dark.

"You'll drive and stay with the van," Slate told Maura. "I want Singer up close in case we need firepower or Briggs makes a run for it out the back door. We don't know as much as we'd like, so we have to plan for the worst. We can watch the house from the trees before moonrise to see whether Briggs has company. If he doesn't, we still have to be careful about alarm systems. Our biggest advantage is that Briggs expects men.

"If we're lucky, we can get in and out and no one will notice. The nearest neighbor is a hundred fifty feet away, so even if we make some noise, I don't expect anybody to call the cops. When we get our hands on Briggs, don't kill him right away. We need to talk."

An hour before dark, the van rumbled up the maintenance road. Maura had painted gas company logos on white contact paper and stuck them on the doors. From a distance, they'd sell. She stopped short of Briggs's property, keeping the van hidden by a stand of trees. Slate and Singer got out to recon.

They crouched in the trees and Slate studied the big picture while Singer took in details with binoculars. The house was huge, built in a style Slate recognized as Tudor, although he doubted the Tudors had an attached garage. The back door was centered on the ground floor and twenty feet to the right, another modern touch, sliding glass doors opened onto a patio. The photograph of the front showed the main door. The banded oak planks were probably a veneer, but for a werewolf, breaking it down shouldn't be a problem if the door was the real deal.

Smoke plumed at the far end of the house. "Fire in the fireplace."

"Guess we don't go down the chimney."

A door at the back of the garage made a fourth way in or out. Lots of doors and windows to watch.

"Uh oh, "Singer said. "Upstairs far left window. It's open."

"And?"

"It's twenty degrees out here. We're sucking ice cubes so our breath doesn't steam. I'm betting—yeah. Take a look." He handed the binoculars to Slate.

Leaning against the sill inside the bedroom Slate saw the fore stock and barrel of a rifle tipped with the thin cylinder of a silencer. "So much for sneaking up from behind."

"Even in the dark?"

"Come on, man, this is the Company. He'll have a star scope or goggles."

"I'll handle him."

"You can't shoot him from here. You'd have to be in the open to hit him. He's in that window so you're a target and he isn't. In the full moon, you'll be as visible as you would be now."

"Let me worry about that."

"We can move through the neighbor's woodlot 'til we're all but thirty degrees out of his sight line, but he's in the house, so he'll have to go anyway. Take him out and the show begins."

LXXXII

MacDonald felt as if a fine wire were stretched through him like a violin string and it hummed with tension. He was on his third cup of coffee in the last hour.

"Bennies?" Theta had said, offering him a bottle of dark capsules.

Mac declined the offer, afraid of what may have really been in them. They were going to kill him, he was sure of that, but why wait to do it? If they needed another gun, they'd have left his bullets in the clip. He knew Slate and his team; that's why Briggs put him on the search in the first place. Was Briggs keeping him close to see whose side he was on? Whatever the reason, Mac knew that as Briggs put it, his ass was on the line.

He realized that if he tried to escape, he wouldn't get fifty feet before they shot him. Mac had to wear his game face and not let on that he knew his gun was empty. As soon as they knew he knew, he'd lose his relative freedom and any chance of getting out alive.

As he drank his coffee, his eye drifted across the kitchen to a knife rack over the sink, one blade, in particular, a foot-long carving knife with a stag handle. If he could get it up his sleeve, maybe he could use it on Briggs before the Dream Team got him. It was worth a try.

LXXXIII

The sunset and the winter sky was dark and clear. Away from the city, the stars came out in greater numbers than Maura had seen since she was on the steppes in Asia. A glow on the horizon portended the rising of the moon. The team crouched under blankets. Singer wore a black coverall and a web belt with canvas pouches around his waist. He held the butt of a long rifle against his left hip, the strap wrapped around his forearm.

"You do your little fandango and then we'll move in," Slate said. "I just hope your idea works."

"It'll work."

"Give us five minutes to get in position at the front of the house."

"Will do." He looked at his watch. "Here comes the Moon."

Moonrise.

Maura spoke the incantation and the *farkas ostor* glowed violet. The change was quiet, peaceful in fact and over quickly. Slate gave a signal and he, Swede, and Haines disappeared silently into the trees.

Maura climbed into the van and waited, hand on the ignition key, ready to drive away at a second's notice. Singer took his position at the edge of the trees fifty yards below the house and pulled down his mask. In his right hand, he held a coffee can full of broken glass.

LXXXIV

Briggs sat in the study in front of the fireplace staring into the flames, smiling. He's enjoying this, thought Mac. He's like a kid playing with toy soldiers. Gamma stood three feet away from him where he could see the whole study in the large mirror over the mantel. Mac sat across the room in a wing chair, too far from Briggs to move on him without Gamma stopping him. The carving knife would make a good close in weapon, but it was too unbalanced to throw. Just wait, he thought. Watch for a chance.

Upstairs Kappa was guarding the back of the property. The moon was just edging over the horizon and soon it would light the back of the grounds well enough that he wouldn't need the night vision goggles that painted the shadowy landscape green.

A dark blip moved across his vision followed by the sound of breaking glass. He swung the rifle toward the noise and in the green glow saw a coffee can clearly enough to read the name Maxwell House on the side.

Suddenly a burst of white light from a phosphorous flare, amplified by the goggles blazed into his eyes, blinding him. Singer broke cover and sprinted across the yard to stand with the flare beside him. Kappa fired wildly at the unseen target. Bullets kicked up dirt all around Singer, but none scored a hit. In the white light from the flare, he saw Kappa framed in the upstairs window. He raised his rifle. Singer needed only one shot.

In the front, Theta crouched in the bushes camouflaged by a ghillie suit, but Slate and Swede didn't need to see him; the scent of his sweat, the Neat's-foot oil on his boots and the onions he'd put on his hamburger a few hours before gave him away.

The tops of the pines changed from black to green in an instant, and Theta saw movement to his left. He brought his M-16 around and peered into the trees. To his right, he heard a snort of breath and he turned in time to see two sets of claws and a mouth full of fangs headed for his throat. He never had the chance to scream.

When the light from the flare blazed through the study windows, Briggs leapt from his chair. Gamma keyed the two-way radio. "Kappa, report. What the hell's going on back there?"

Mac got to his feet and started edging toward Briggs. Gamma's pistol appeared from nowhere. He gestured with it to Mac. "You, come with me." He turned to Briggs. "Sir, stay here 'til we see what's what." He keyed the radio. "Theta, report. Theta, where are you?"

Gamma pushed Mac ahead of him around the corner into the hallway, leaving Briggs alone in the study. Then Theta's headless body crashed through the window with Slate right behind it.

At the front, Swede hurtled against the door. It didn't break; it was real. But it came off the hinges and fell inward with a crash. Delta was waiting in the darkened entrance hallway in a shooter's stance with a .45 automatic. He instinctively fired a standard triangle of shots into the invader's chest before the dark furred monster cleared the doorway. The creature kept coming. Delta stared into its glowing yellow eyes and panic fired until the clip was empty.

Swede brought a paw like a clawed first baseman's mitt upward in an arc that caught Delta under his flak vest and tore the vest away along with most of his ribcage.

Haines threw a concrete planter through the patio doors and dove through the maw of jagged glass. As he ran into the kitchen, he heard the sound of metal rolling across the tiled floor. A bright flash and a concussion took Haines off his feet.

The stun grenade was agony to his heightened senses. Haines pushed himself up to his hands and knees and shook his head to clear it. He raised his eyes to see Gamma coming at him with the hooked blade of a Gurkha knife poised to sweep his head off with a single stroke. Haines rolled to the side and threw up an arm to block the wicked blade. Gamma missed his throat, but two of Haines's clawed fingers flew across the kitchen, cut so cleanly he didn't feel the pain at first.

Gamma swung again, but his swing went wild as Mac came up behind him and drove the carving knife into one side of his throat and out the other. Gamma lurched wide-eyed and staggered toward Mac, knife raised for a killing stroke, but a swipe of Haines's paw swept Gamma's feet from under him. The assassin crashed face down on the floor. Haines leapt onto Gamma's back and drove a bone crushing fist into the back of his neck.

Haines got unsteadily to his feet and in the dim light from the doorway, MacDonald saw the intruder for the first time. He stared at the fanged horror and was too terrified to run.

Haines's chest heaved. He growled a deep menacing sound. In a guttural voice, he said, "Mac." Then with a backhanded swipe, he knocked MacDonald to the floor unconscious.

Haines grabbed MacDonald by his jacket and dragged him down the hallway toward the sound of voices. Swede padded down the stairs, claws ticking on the hardwood treads. "Clear," he snarled.

"Clear outside," Singer said, coming through the front doorway. They went into the study to find Briggs in an armchair with Slate's clawed fingers holding him by the throat.

Briggs's eyes darted wildly from Slate to the others. "I'll be damned. It's not a costume. You're for real."

"As real as a heart attack," said Singer. "You know why we're here."

Briggs snorted. "Tyler and Hitchcock. Some deluded code of honor, right? Wake up. There is no honor, no justice, no right and wrong, just raw power and the hand that steers it."

"Who else?" snarled Slate.

"The buck stops here," said Briggs, and he let out a manic burst of laughter.

Slate turned to Singer. "You first," he growled.

He pulled a double edged dagger from his boot. "This is for Tyler." He drove the knife to the hilt into Briggs's gut. Briggs gritted his teeth and roared in pain. "And this is for Faro." Singer plunged the knife into Briggs's chest to the left of his breastbone, careful to miss his heart. He pulled out the blade and wiped it on the sleeve of Briggs's baby blue sweater.

Briggs's breath wheezed through the hole in his lung. Singer stepped back. All three of the werewolves dug their claws into Briggs and tore away his flesh until there was little left of him but a skeleton.

Singer found Haines's fingers in the kitchen and brought them into the study. He picked up Briggs's fluted champagne glass and dropped them into it. "I'll get some ice from the refrigerator. Maybe they'll heal if we can get them sewn back on. At least it's not your trigger finger."

MacDonald woke tied to a chair. He stared at the werewolves then his gaze fixed on Singer. "Hello, Mac." Singer walked around him as if studying him from all angles. "It's a lot to take in all at once, I know. Welcome to reality."

Slate crouched before Mac, staring into his eyes. MacDonald's eyes widened. Slate turned to the others. "Take him outside." Swede and Haines lifted Mac, chair and all and walked out the front door.

Slate reached into the fireplace and grabbed one of the andirons and yanked it free, spilling the blazing logs onto the carpet. "Time to go."

Outside, Mac saw the flames through the window. "Well go on," said Mac. "Just kill me and get it over with.

"Oh no, Mac," Slate said in his bestial voice. "We won't kill you. We need a job."

LXXXV

"Virginia," said Greystone, his finger poised over the map.

"Shall I go after them?" Mister Smith said. His arm hung in a sling.

"Not yet. Let us wait a bit to see whether they have learned to not allow lightning to hit the same tree twice."

LXXXVI

Outside Gatlinburg, Tennessee, Singer pulled the van into the parking lot of Doctor Ben Sawyer's veterinary hospital. It was one-thirty and everything was dark, both the animal hospital on the ground floor and the doctor's residence above.

Singer didn't really need to knock on the door. The animals inside were raising holy hell, sensing the presence of the werewolves outside. Sawyer, a crotchety old widower came to the door in a nightshirt over trousers and bare feet. He opened it and peered at Singer and Maura through rimless glasses.

"We have an emergency," Singer said.

Sawyer opened his mouth to speak but before he could, Haines stepped between Singer and Maura, holding out his injured hand. "Help me, please," he snarled.

"Holy Mother of God," said Sawyer and tried to close the door.

Singer got a foot in it and put his pistol under Sawyer's nose. "You'll meet her a lot sooner than you want unless you take us to your treatment room now."

Haines stretched out on a stainless steel table big enough for a Doberman but too short for his legs which hung over the end from the knees. Singer handed the champagne glass with Haines's fingers in it to Sawyer. "Sew them back on."

Sawyer stared at the monster on the table and stammered, "It, it'll hurt like the devil. What if he . . ."

"He won't harm you," said Maura. "Just do it."

Sawyer despite shaking hands, reattached both of Haines's fingers and wrapped them tightly with gauze and tape. "That should hold them."

Singer came up behind Sawyer and gave him a short punch just under his jaw. Sawyer slumped to the floor. Singer pulled a hypodermic needle and a small ampoule from his pocket and began filling the syringe.

"You're going to kill him?" Maura said.

Singer shook his head. "No, just send him away for a while."

"What's in the hypo?"

"Lysergic acid diethylamide."

"LSD?"

"Enough to make him think it's all been a dream." He pushed in the plunger and said, "I'll get Mikey out to the van. You turn out the lights."

LXXXVII

The table was set for Thanksgiving dinner. Billy could smell the turkey all the way from the driveway where he was shooting hoops.

"Billy," his mother called from the kitchen window, "phone for you."

He set the basketball in the grass beside the garage and went inside.

"Hello?"

"Hi, Billy."

"Roxy, uh hi."

"Just wanted to let you know, *Unidentified* is going to run the story in two weeks. Happy Thanksgiving. How's it feel to be the turkey?"

LXXXVIII

Maura sat on the overlook, feet over the edge, staring down into the chasm at the river. Thanksgiving. I should be thankful, she thought. I'm still alive and I've learned more in the last two weeks than I have in a lifetime of research, but there's a price; always a price. She had called a friend the day before to check on her apartment and move her car. That's when she learned that Robert Mansoor was dead.

"Some jerk ran him over with a car in a little town in Georgia. Paper said it was an accident; hit-and-run." It was no accident, Maura thought. Intuition told her it was the tall man who attacked her for the *farkas ostor* in the swamp, though she had no way to know for sure.

Footsteps behind her. She turned and saw Singer coming across the limestone ledge. He sat beside her and pulled out his cigarettes. He lit two and handed one to Maura. "How are you doing?"

"I'm all right. The last two weeks have been a lot to swallow, that's all."

"I guess so. It took me a while to get used to the werewolf thing."

"It's not just that. It's the whole scene, the CIA, the wizards, the — what did you call them — black bag operations. I had no idea."

"Most people don't. If they did, they'd pull the Capitol down stone by stone and be justified to do it. But as long as they don't know, life goes on as usual. It hasn't been any different since ancient Rome, maybe before that."

"Even the magic?"

Singer stared into the ravine. "I heard stories about a special squad in the OSS in World War II that used magic against the Nazis. I thought it was bunk 'til now."

Neither spoke for a while. Below them, the river flowed on. Singer stubbed out his cigarette. "So how about you? What's next?"

"I don 't know. I guess there's no rush to decide. My sabbatical runs for another nine months. And I'm not even sure I can go back to that life. There's no way I could ever publish what I've learned. You'd all be compromised and I'd be marked. That man in the swamp was only one. There'll be others. Besides that I helped you kill five people, CIA people. There's no doubt what they'd do to me if they found me. I'm safer with you guys than anywhere."

"Still in for a buck, huh?"

"And change."

Singer put a hand between her shoulder blades. He looked over his shoulder where Slate stood half hidden in a stand of mountain laurel. Slate shook his head, turned and slipped away. Singer patted her back. "You'll be fine. Welcome to the pack."

THE END

ABOUT OUR CREATORS

AUTHOR –

FRED ADAMS - is a western Pennsylvania native who has enjoyed a lifelong love affair with horror, fantasy, and science fiction literature and films. He holds a Ph.D. in American Literature from Duquesne University and recently retired from teaching writing and literature in the English Department of Penn State University.

He has published over 50 short stories in amateur, and professional magazines as well as hundreds of news features as a staff writer and sportswriter for the now Pittsburgh Tribune-Review. In the 1970s Fred published the fanzine Spoor and its companion The Spoor Anthology. Hitwolf, Six-Gun Terror, and Dead Man's Melody were his three first books for Airship 27 is his first, and his nonfiction book, Edith Wharton's American Gothic: Gods, Ghosts, and Vampires will be published by Borgo Press in 2014.

INTERIOR ILLUSTRATOR -

CLAYTON HINKLE - is a life-long, self-taught (for the most part) artist whose main ambition in life is to basically draw cool, adventurous, fantastic, horrific, Pulp and Comic art. Most, if not all, of his published work, has been in the new Pulps of today, Air Ship 27 Productions being the major outlet of his wares by far, as well as work for the fanzine "REH, Two-Gun Raconteur", a 'zine dedicated to the late, great Robert E. Howard and his works. He hopes to one day make his living by drawing, pure and simple.

Cover Artist-

ZACHARY BRUNNER – graduated from the School of Arts with a degree in filmmaking. Upon graduation, he realized that he would rather pursue a career in illustration, needing a more creative job than the high-stress environment of film production. He began working with comic writer Jim Krueger on two graphic novels, "The High Cost of Happily Ever After," and "Runner." Both are currently available at Amazon.

While studying at SVA, Zachary worked as a concept artist on an animated film called "Brother," directed by Sari Rodrig. The short film went on to win countless awards all over the world, having been shown at festivals such as Cannes and the Student Emmys. Zach currently is working on Sari's second short animated film, "Essence." For the past year, he has also worked as a storyboard artist for Torque Creative, the in-house advertising agency for Mercedes-Benz. He is also currently working on several storyboards for short independent films. Other print projects included "Christopher Rising," "Penny Dreadful" and "The Poisonberry Fortune" and "Foot Soldiers,Volume 1." He plans on furthering a career in concept art and in the comic book industry.

THE WAYS OF MAGIC

During World War II, C.O. Jones, under a different name, was recruited into a special unit of the OSS (Office of Strategic Services). Special in that all the members had some kind of extrasensory abilities bordering on magic. Their main mission was to seek out and combat the Nazis' top secret Occult Practioners.

But the war is now over and C.O. is just another veteran looking for a fresh start. He hopes the quiet little town of Brownsville, Pennsylvania is the perfect place to do so. That is, until he gets involved with the local criminal element and discovers, through his own unique gifts, that someone is using dark magic to further their own illegal agenda. For C.O. Jones, it seems the ways of magic are to be found in the most unlikely places.

Popular new pulp writer Fred Adams, Jr. delivers another scorching thriller that races across the pages with fresh, original characters, suspense and ever-exploding action. Hold on to your seatbelts as you meet the C.O. Jones, one of the toughest new pulp heroes of them all.

AN AIRSHIP 27 PRODUCTION
AIRSHIP27HANGAR.COM
NEW PULP

C.O. JONES

MOBSTERS & MONSTERS
FRED ADAMS JR.

PULP FICTION FOR A NEW GENERATION!